HEALER NEST

By

Margaret Afseth

Amazon/kindle Edition

Copyright 2014 by Margaret Afseth

ISBN: 978-1-927828-47-2

Publisher's note: This novel is a work of fiction. Names, characters, places and incidents are either products of the author's imagination or used fictitiously. All characters are fictional, and similarity to people living or dead purely coincidental.

This book is dedicated to my oncology care providers. Michelle, you gave me a hug when I was down; Hui, you watched over me at night, and Doctor Assem(Awesome), you were the most gentle physician I have ever met. Thank you for getting me through the hardest time of my life.

I created Loki before I ever met Doctor Assem, and it shocked me to actually find someone that mirrored my character. This last of the series was written while this author was sight impaired, and recovering from chemo and radiation therapy.

Table of Contents

PROLOGUE:

With the help of a sleep teaching disk, Bom upgraded his education in computer board programs, and noxious substances. He already was sufficiently familiar with advanced Roog weaponry.

His diminutive personal ship was completely automated. He knew enough of its operation to take it alone into deep space, through Jumper Central, and reach any destination in a matter of days. And though he could not operate it, the bay of his ship also contained a fair sized shuttle for his convenience.

Approaching Dia's enormous city-size emergency treatment facility was exceptionally easy. Bom was a registered Feline, even though he was half Roog; of a race that was their mortal enemy. But, the system simply accepted him.

As yet, they have not blocked me, though that will certainly change after this night's actions. But, by then, what I wish to accomplish will be done, I will be long gone, and it will no longer matter.

Uncontested, he slid his mini ship into a dock in the cavernous bay, and hit the image on his screen to power down.

As soon as he entered the med ship proper, Bom went straight to their mainframe. Most were on sleep break, which meant a skeleton staff. No one challenged him.

He went in with the password he'd set up from an outside terminal. It was in his father's name, who supposedly had access to all and any data, in any frame, because of his station as head of the Universal council.

It was easy to shut down inter-ship communications, and drop the shields on Dia's home nest. Even her Slither sentries were unaware of the change; that their charges were now vulnerable to outside attack.

Then he introduced the canister of the powerful sedative, he'd brought with him from his ship; fed it directly into the ventilation system, and donned an artificial breather.

After waiting the allotted time for the drug to take effect, he shut down the Noor energy ceiling in Dia's sleep room. Remotely, Bom blanketed the area with the drain beam weapon aboard his ship.

The whole thing went so well. The corridor door opened easily to his touch. When he arrived at the chamber, the Slither guards were visible, unconscious on the floor.

Using medic drones, who were programmed with the code for an emergency, he easily entered the sanctum of Dia, and transported the incapacitated Noor to his docked ship.

But, he had taken too long. Even though his prisoners were now shackled, and in drain belts, with a drain beam blanketing the compartment where they were held, he never knew what Loki's she was capable of.

And, he had one more need to fill.

I need a shuttle pilot! For that last distance to the moon cavern, I can't use the jump portal. Too many hostages now. Never knew they had accumulative so much family! And I only took those with the headbands...

Bom strode through the silent corridors of the single-warrior sleep-chambers, searching for one who would fit his criteria. There was no time left to pick and choose among these unconscious occupants.

Can't be certain, the one I pick, can operate a shuttle...

And, someone might awaken, and discover what he had done.

At just that moment the intercom sounded.

I must have missed a backup system!

"Alert! Alert!" came Thor's angry voice. "The ship contains intruders! The air is filled with poison. Close off the circulation vents! Flush the system!"

Enough of this! I need one of the captain's crew!

Bom spun on his heel, and headed at a lope, for the nearest lift. He hoped they wouldn't be clear thinking enough to shut those down just yet.

On the upper deck, the mixed breed creature found the slumped, still unconscious figures of five Feline minor officers; one was a skinny, pure white, long haired, younger male, perhaps, in his late twenties, obviously an apprentice. But Bom knew, if he was on the command deck, they had already trained him to operate both the larger vessel, as well as a shuttle.

He'll not have had much practice, but...he'll have to do.

And...he should stay out for a bit longer. He's not so large...will have ingested more of the drug.

Slinging the unfortunate trainee to his shoulder, Bom took off hurriedly to the down elevator, descending rapidly to the bowels, where his ship was docked.

****

At the age of two thousand and one, Kei needed her many naps more so than any other Feline in the species. She awoke now, instantly alert, blinking fearfully, panic coursing through her system.

She had had a most terrifying vision!

Kei had dreamed: that the Noor Queen, and all her clan, had been incarcerated; the one she'd chosen to take her place would now never head the twelve Feline planets, nor rescue the Universe from the rule of the devil dogs. The plight of all was sealed by order of Clio, the Roog head of the Universal council, and his mixed breed son, Bom. With all the Noor in captivity, there was no one to thwart the desires of these two bestial foes.

The Feline proxy ruler trembled, her body shaking visibly.

It can't be true. I won't believe it! It was merely a nightmare, brought on by undigested food.

Besides, if such a thing has happened, the end result is not a done deal. The Maker of us all has plans for her. It will not let it end like this!

****

The atmosphere of the middle world, in the twelve planet system, seemed suddenly to hold its breath. Then abruptly space split, and the area about the enormous globe was filled with enemy ships, materializing as if from thin air. Huge monster battle craft, resembling the dogs that piloted them, surrounded the seat of Feline government on all sides.

But this region is said to be protected! How did they slipped into Feline space, so close and undetected? Had they stolen the technology from the very peoples they were now threatening? Who betrayed the Feline species?

Bom? Or his father, Clio?

****

A male sentry, the fated messenger, risking his own death, burst into the sacrosanct chambers of his Monarch. The huge guardian warrior, beside the cot where she reclined, turned, on instant alert, claws extended, spitting viciously.

"Easy," the old female warned, sitting up. "Stand down! Give him time; he means me no harm."

Then waving for the panting intruder to come forward, she addressed him.

"What is the meaning of this unscheduled entry into my presence? Your message had best be of vital importance, or I will let my protector have at you."

"My Lady," he gasped. "The planet is surrounded by enemy ships...the dogs..."

Kei did not wait for another word. She turned to the warrior at her side.

"Summon the superintendent of evacuation...No!" she decided, abruptly changing her mind, as she realized there was too little time. "Tell him...begin to transport the females, their partners, and their families to other safe systems. He is to use all available jump portals, and to proceed with the utmost haste. We need to save as many as possible..."

"You must be the first, my Lady," ventured her guardian. But she immediately disagreed.

"Their purpose in choosing this planet first, is to cut off the head, so that the limbs will be without direction, and therefore, they think, useless. But, as always, they have underestimated us. I am ruler no longer...only the proxy."

Stunned, the two males present looked at her speechless for a second.

"My Lady?" finally ventured the one who had so rudely burst in. "What say you?"

"The Monarchy has been passed to my successor some time ago. She wished me to remain as proxy, as a means of deception, and it has worked. Now that the Roog have finally shown their hand, I see it as a wise decision. But, to the matter at hand. Why do you hesitate? Lives are in the balance!"

As her guardian went to the computer wall board to carry out her wishes, the one who remained behind probed further:

"But Lady. Where then is our real Sovereign?"

Kei smiled. "Pass the word, young warrior. The twelve planets are not crippled, even should I die. You will all know, when you find the one you seek. Use your logic; and it is on record... fight now! We are at war with the devil dogs! Protect the real Queen!"

"But you, my Lady. What will become of you?"

"I am old; I have lived a long and delightful life. I will not regret my passing...go, young one. Leave me, now."

****

Tzachok opened his blue eyes with great difficulty. It seemed in their lack of focus, he was seeing double.

"So, you are finally awake," growled a deep voice.

Tza yelped when he could finally see the huge form crouched before him. Even as a young kit, the half dog creature had frightened him, and he would run and hide, leaving his elders to deal with Bom.

The small Feline gagged at the odor that reeked off his subjugator's body, for the mixed breed male was none too clean. He was not inclined to wash his fur, as other Feline did. Nor was he pleasant to look at, either.

His bulldog-like visage was pure canine, a dark black with tan markings. The ears flopped over, instead of standing up, and were rounded at the ends, unlike the pointy ears of other Feline. His features resembled his Roog father, Clio, and like him, he had the vicious predatory nature.

But, his body was that of a cat; long black course fur, matted bushy tail, and deadly claws.

Bom stood up, his heavy build and eight foot height towering menacingly.

"Well, get up! I have work for you to do."

Tza swallowed convulsively. He knew there was no point trying to fight this beast, so he followed submissively after him.

Bom led him to the controls of a shuttle.

"Fly me down to the surface."

The younger Feline took his seat.

As they escaped the bay of the larger ship, Tza found he was nowhere near home. Far away he saw a blue and green planet; one he'd often seen on the simulator screen, for they used the Forbidden planet as the target in all training.

Oh, Almighty Maker, am I going to Bom's dungeon prison? What have I done to deserve this?

But Bom interrupted his thoughts. "Steer us to the dark side of its moon."

Tza breathed a sigh of relief.

Perhaps there is hope, after all.

But as he came around to the valley on the dark side, in closer to the surface, there beneath him was a cavernous holding bay, leading into the bowels of the rock. He landed, and powered down.

Tzachok thought his job was over now, but Bom was not yet finished with him.

"Come; we have to hurry, before they wake up on me."

When Tza saw the prisoners, in the shuttle's holding cells, his spirit plummet drastically. Bom had all members of the mighty Healer clan, even the youngest female, Kaudy, in torture drain-belts, and shackle chains. Hand and foot, they were hobbled, near bent double, so they couldn't move; still unconscious, and drained of energy. The mighty Noor were helpless, and there was nothing he could do to set them free.

Tza began to keen in fearful dread of the fate that awaited them.

"Shut up!" bellowed Bom, cuffing him alongside the head. "What good are you, if you are going to whine like that?"

The young Feline went to his knees, sobbing uncontrollably.

"If I didn't need your help, I'd end your miserable life right now, you poor excuse of a cat moron!" Then it seemed to dawn on the cruel beast just why Tzachok was so upset. "So...you don't like to see them like this? Well, what if I kill one of them before your very eyes? How would you like that?"

Reason was not a factor in Tza's choice; he actually hoped he might deter the end result. He dried his tears, stood up, and waited for further instructions.

"We'll take Loki first. Which one is he?"

Not often had Tza actually seen the Noor junction males, but Liam had rescued him as a young kit, and also been on the bridge when the young male had been introduced to the crew. He knew which twin wasn't Loki.

Puzzled, by the fact that Bom couldn't tell them apart, even though Loki had spent time in his prison dungeons, Tza pointed to the correct brother.

"Okay! I have something special for him. Grab his feet."

Their burden was exceedingly heavy, for Loki weighed close to six hundred pounds, but the dark tunnels they passed through were mostly downhill.

At last, the two panting males, with their load, arrived at a room that was equipped as a chamber of torture. Among the tools of torment was a miniature bared cage, bolted deep into the stone floor.

Bom unceremoniously dropped his end of the burden. The unconscious Noor's head cracked against the hard granite, resoundingly, and Tza winced in sympathy, for the headache Loki would have when he awoke.

The giant Roog/Feline swung open the small door to the four foot square, by six foot high cage.

"Put him inside," Bom ordered, pointing. "And make it quick. I'll be back shortly..."

"But...it's too small for him in there," objected Tza.

"Exactly," laughed Bom. "But you can do it. The door will lock when you shut it."

Bom was back with Liam, before Tza had accomplished his sordid task. The evil creature ignored the young male, until he had strapped the unconscious Liam to the wall in an X formation, by bands at his ankles, wrists and throat. He spun the wall, and the naked form of the second twin disappeared behind the partition.

Then, Bom came with a lock and chain, wrapped them through the bars of Loki's cage, and around the door frame, then padlocked the ends.

If ever Tza was able to bring help, he wondered how they would ever get the Noor free.

While Bom had him hauling the younger Noor, and confining them in another room, Tza racked his brain, mulling over different scenarios in which they might be set free.

The last prisoner, Liam/Loki's beautiful bride, was chained by the neck, to the stone floor of the room that contained the cage.

Then Bom lead Tza back to the shuttle.

"You are just going to leave them there?" Tza ventured. "They don't even have a light source. They'll die!"

"Oh, I'm not finished yet! I'll bring them around later," Bom declared. "First, need to deal with the shuttle. Take us back to my ship."

As they stepped from the shuttle to the metal floor of the larger ship, before Tzachok had a chance to think of fleeing, his huge antagonist grabbed him by the scruff of his neck. Suspended so, Bom literally carried the younger Feline to his onboard transport pad.

Next thing, they were back underground again.

I am next!

Tza whined plaintively. He let go the contents of his bladder, embarrassing himself. But Bom was not the least sympathetic, only disgusted by the dribbling, dripping, wimp of a creature in his paw.

Bom roped him by the neck to a wall in a far away room, bound his paws and feet, then turned to leave the room. As he left, Tza found his bravado; he suddenly had no qualms at demanding an accounting from the devil dog/cat.

"When have I ever wronged you, Bom? What is my crime, that you sentence me to such a death of shame?"

Bom growled deep in his throat. "You served Dia, and her half Noor clan! That is offense enough in my father's world. You are nothing to me! You have served a purpose. Now, I have better things to torture...more fun than playing with you. Be thankful. You will still have a slow death by starvation."

And then he was gone, leaving Tza to deal with his fright, and regretful thoughts.

****

Across the regions of space, around the Feline seat of government, the ships just sat there. For days, by their very presence, they threatened the Feline peoples below. Then, as suddenly as they'd come, they vanished.

Shortly thereafter, the massive world was rocked by a chain reaction of subterranean explosions. The Roog had jumped demolition experts, deep into the caverns beneath the surface, where they had planted charges, set to go off, just after the Roog had left Feline space.

The shock wave from the blast that tore this vital world apart, hit the next planet in line just after noon the next day, but by then, those on it had been warned, and shields, and buffers were up.

All females from home world had been saved...all save one. With the one remaining warrior, who would not leave her side, Kei lingered behind until all were safe. Before she could step to the transporter pad behind her faithful guardian, the planet exploded.

And so at her death, began a battle like no other; for supremacy over the entire known Universe. As Kei had requested, the bearer of the original ill tidings, spread her message across the Universal battlefields, from ship to ship:

Felines are fighting for their new Sovereign! And we will find her, no matter where the Roog have taken her!

Chapter 1

When the giant dogs began to hunt exclusively above the ground, it seemed nature, even the very planet, had sided with the Roog to expel, and annihilate human kind.

Volcanic eruptions filled the air with powdered ash, leaving continual grey smog across the globe for daylight hours. Sulfur fumes spewed into the atmosphere, killing nearby vegetation, and turning the air toxic, in the close vicinity of eruptions. In the northern hemisphere there was unusual cooling, while in the south, stifling heat.

The ground shook from constant earthquakes, as tectonic plates moved and shifted. Unstable buildings fell against others, trapping inhabitants under the rubble. Those unharmed by the tremors, or the devastation, found themselves homeless; lacking food; their water contaminated.

But their worst fears were realized in the nocturnal hours. As they sat in their makeshift shelters, waiting for rescue, they were easy prey for monster predators.

From the few who made it through the first nights, the world soon learned the name of the vicious invaders. Death by them was brutal; these creatures spared no one. Some they tore limb from limb, eating them alive on the spot; others were taken with them, to feed upon later.

The Roog were dogs of huge stature, many over seven feet tall; malicious and bestial in nature. Some resembled Bulldogs or Boxers, others Dobermans or Rottweilers; most every breed of dog was represented in one form or another. But the worse factor was, they seemed to have a malevolent and deliberate intelligence to them. They walked erect, balancing on their hind limbs, and wore simple garments; it was rumored, they even spoke in the tongue of their captives. And though it was not proven, it was said some even carried a form of laser weapon.

At first it was thought, the Roog only appeared in the third world countries, areas ravished by quakes, volcanic eruptions, mudslides, or floods. The predators avoided the water, and it was in the rivers, some humans seemed to find safety...at least for a time. Directly, it was found, the Roog could swim; they simply preferred not to; to wait out their prey. It was a game that aroused them.

As foreign help arrived, bringing civilian attempts at aid for the unfortunates, and confident army protection set up for the nights, camera crews followed, spreading across the globe a view, live, of the giant intruders as they came. Unless you were unfortunate enough to be their prey, this was the last sight mankind would see of the Dog hunters on camera, as by morning the entire inhabitants of the refugee camp, all army, rescue, and media personal had vanished.

It was thought the more affluent countries were free of the menace, but that proved not to be the case. Each disaster, whether hurricane, tornado, fire, earthquake, or other forms of natural storm; no matter the location on the globe; city or countryside; as catastrophe struck causing devastation, injury, and death, at night the very ground seemed to vomit giant dogs, to hunt those who were helpless. It was as if they oozed from the soil.

Whole areas were not only devastated by natural disasters, but picked clean of humanity. When morning came, the streets were empty, not only absent of the cruel enemy, but missing all other residents; even the police and army personal sent to help.

In most large cities, a curfew was soon strictly enforced for darkness hours; martial law was proclaimed, and army personal took to guarding the people at night. Using every weapon at their disposal, military patrols went after the huge animals, yet it appeared they were crafty, able to avoid easily. They seemed to vanish as if into thin air, and the more Roog humans killed, the more the hunters increased.

It spread from city to city, that not only could the beasts talk, they were organized, and had use of transportation, gathering people into trucks and huge vans. Where the captives were taken was never discovered; though roadblocks were set up, even the vehicles were never seen again in the vicinity.

In the cities and towns unaffected, life continued in an almost normal fashion. The people were anxious, but most disbelieved the tale being told by the media, believing it to be a gimmick to raise ratings. Every night, the talk show hosts discussed the recent cell phone video footage sent into the station. Most often, the sender was never heard from again.

Many people cowed in their homes at night, fearing the worst, that their city would be next, their private sanctuary invaded. And so, the remnants of humanity hid, went out only during daylight hours, barred their door at night, and took shifts standing guard with guns.

Transportation soon suffered. Truckers were reluctant to head out on long hauls that involved over night travel; rail cars ran straight through without stopping, because the stations were unmanned. Flying by air became a thing of the past, as no pilot or passenger wanted to be caught out after dark.

Food became a precious commodity; if you had a garden you were subject to thieves unless you were walled in. Mall grocers and corner stores were often without adequate supplies, raising the costs exuberantly.

Society began to break down, but only the very bravest of demonstrators dared criticize their governments for inaction. Rioting was not even considered; for even burglars dare not leave their homes at night.

Yet, as always, somehow, the wealthy had sufficient supplies. Those connected to government had an abundance; the professionals always ate well; while the underprivileged perished...unless they were resourceful.

Chapter 2

When the second world war began, Tia's grandfather had gone to Ottawa to enlist in the Canadian army as an interpreter. He was one of the few accepted.

At that time, he had no right to vote or own a business. All Japanese were suspect in those days, as the attack on Pearl Harbor had turned many against even the innocent Canadian Japanese citizen.

Because he had also died on the battlefield, along with thousands of other Japanese Canadians, his farm and all property was confiscated, sold by the government; the family ejected from Canada, and shipped off to Japan.

By the time Tia was born in 1993, things were very much better for her family, though the shame of the past still rode the shoulders of her father. Manzo had gotten a derisory settlement for the war time criminal wrongs, and unlike most Japanese who rightfully belonged in Canada, but refused to return, he had come back to the place of his birth with his aged mother, Midi, unmarried sister, Kerri, and his Japanese born wife, Kim.

With their compensation, Manzo had bought a large duplex on the prairies, and started a computer supply business in one of the major cities. He was now retired, and Tomekichi, his son, was head of the household; the business he ran, the sole provision for the family.

The family had increased. Tomekichi, named for his grandfather, had taken a Canadian born wife, Joy, and was the proud father of Jack, two, and Naomi, one year. And of course, Tia had come along ten years after the birth of the heir.

Tia was expected to join her brother in the business, which had expanded to computer programming. She was presently in college, training to that end.

They still lived in the duplex, but it had been renovated to suit a Japanese household. Both upper and lower floor rooms were interconnected; the top floor for Tommy's family and Tia; the ground floor for Grandmother, now ninety-six; Father and Mother, and Father's sixty-two year old younger sister.

The small kitchen, dining area, and bath were communal. The three bathrooms had been combined creating a spacious three room unit consisting of: the entrance room, where one washed hands, undressed and sponged off; the room for the soaking tub and shower; and off to the side, by itself, the room for the stool.

As Japanese, the family was always well aware their fortunes could change in a matter of seconds, but they had never bargained on a world situation such as existed at the moment. As Tia took her courses, going back and forth from the college, she was careful, always, to car pool for safety, and returned home before darkness fell.

****

Tia got off the bus at the transfer depot. She was annoyed that she must take public transport at all, and this leg of the journey would be alone. Her class had gone on longer than expected, and she had missed her ride.

At least, it is mid afternoon. I should still get home before dark.

The glassed-in waiting shelter was occupied by one other. Seated on the bench of her walker, cloth bags of groceries hanging from both handle bars, was an elderly Caucasian woman. She looked to be in her mid eighties, her short grey hair disheveled, and obviously unwashed, as was her body. Tia could smell her unpleasant odor even from a distance.

The woman carried more poundage than was good for her physical frame, which was twisted to one side, as if at some point, she had suffered a stroke.

The sour look on her face seemed meant to discourage conversation, but her eyes held such a haunted look, Tia felt sorry for her, and having been taught social graces, she made the attempt to strike up a conversation.

"My, what beautiful eyes you have."

The woman grunted derisively. "I'm sight impaired; how can my eyes be pretty? Oh," she added. "You are partial to blue eyes, because yours are brown."

Tia let that go; at least it had opened the avenue to communication.

"You shouldn't be out alone. Aren't you afraid you'll be attacked?"

"There was no one to help me," the senior declared caustically. "And I needed groceries."

"Don't you have a husband? Or a son?"

The old woman made a rude sound. "My companion abandoned me. Said, I would have to fend for myself; he was going someplace safe."

Tia gave a quick intake of breath. "Oh, so sorry. What is your name?"

"Pam."

"You are taking an awful chance, Pam. What if you get caught out after dark? Do you not fear the giant dogs?"

Tia fully expected denial that the world wide predators existed at all. She was considerably shocked by the elder's reply.

"They don't dare hurt me! They have no right to plague me. I'm immune! I was with them from the age of ten; gave them over thirty fetuses; then worked kitchen until I couldn't stand. I earned my freedom! They tagged me, and let me live privileged, as a spy. I even gave them an adult female to feast on..."

Tia's frown had deepened with each word.

She's totally insane. Her situation has driven her mad, and she's fabricated this fanatical scenario...poor thing.

"They won't hurt me! I gave them what they needed all those years. I spent a lifetime in their breeding kennels; I earned my freedom! I did! I bear the tag to prove it!"

Tia shook her head, and turned away, just as two young teens joined them in the glass cubicle.

Oh, ya. Definitely not all there.

Tia struck up a new conversation with the most recent arrivals.

"What bus are you waiting for?"

Maybe, I won't be travelling alone, after all.

****

The old duplex creaked at night. It was late, but Tia was still up, reviewing the days lessons.

When she had arrived home, she'd been scolded by Joy, her brother's wife, for being late, causing unnecessary worry. But her reasons for delay were acceptable, and Tia had been reprieved. While her brother soaked away the stress of work, relaxing in the hot water of the programmable tub, Tia was permitted to go and study. Excused from preparing for the meal, as aunt Kerri was already helping, Tia climbed the stairs to her room.

All was quiet now, the communal evening repast finished; the infants settled for the night, and the elders retired. Tia, wanting to have her lessons perfect in her head, for the next day, had returned to her laptop to practice, losing track of time.

The wind moaned through the attic eaves; Tia thought she heard a step upon the stairs.

But no, all are in bed by now.

She decided she was mistaken, and went back to her studies.

From the children's room next door, a muted squeal, choked off abruptly, caught her attention. Listening intently a moment, brought no further sound, so Tia again turned her eyes to her screen.

When she heard Jack's timid, panicked, wail through the wall, Tia shut down her computer, and rose to attend to him, before he woke his parents, in the room across the hall.

Before Tia had a chance to reach the door, a second strident scream rent the air. Then, dead silence...except for a low ominous growling.

Tia's heart jumped to her throat; her pulse began to pound with dread. Yet bravely, she approached the hall door, and opened it.

She was met by a gruesome sight. Just rising up on its hind legs, a monster dog met her, his jaws crimson and dripping with blood.

Tia stifled a scream; backed up to close the door, but the beast reached out and blocked her from doing it. The last thought that went through her head was:

It is too late to save the babies!

Then pandemonium hell broke loose.

Chapter 3

Dia, Feline owner of the city-sized med-ship space-vessel, entered the enormous meeting room filled with personal. Her posture was one of dignity and calm. There was no evidence, on her features, of the grief she was experiencing, only an underlying sense of restrained anger beneath the stoic manner.

The room became hushed, expectant, waiting for her first words.

"By now, most of you know, our home world was attacked by the Roog fleet, and destroyed. Kei, our Queen, is dead!"

For those who were hearing the news for the first time, Dia paused, to let the information sink in.

"The Feline nation is now at war! The Dog creatures have gone too far!"

Again, she paused for emphasis.

"They think, they have the upper hand, but they are sadly mistaken. Just before the blast, the home world was successfully evacuated; all females with their families, and guardians, escaped. And the second planet was forewarned, as well; prepared. It is still intact. We may now have only eleven planets to their extremely overpopulated three, and are thought to be too timid a species to resist, but we do know the meaning of sacrifice. We can be valiant in battle!

"They believe we have no overseer; that we will be in disarray, but they are wrong! Kei did not leave us leaderless! Even before the Roog attacked, our Queen had a premonition; saw a foretelling of what was about to happen. She prepared for her death, appointing a successor."

A murmur of appreciation ran through the crowd. Dia raised a paw for silence.

"Until this moment, my ship has been a place of peace, and safety for all. We turned none away, caring for the sick, and the injured of any species. We have always been neutral! But...No More!"

Her words were met by a shocked silence.

"I have been violated! Robbed of my most prized possession; my children! You have been equally despoiled! Our ship has harbored, and treasured the Instant Healers, and...one reprehensible, traitor has stolen them from us!"

Beneath the podium, anger began to show itself in hisses of displeasure. Dia waited for the din to die down, then continued.

"I have always accepted those who did not fit in elsewhere: the half ones; those of mixed genus. But Bom, the one who is responsible for taking my family, though he be a cross-breed, is no longer welcome. He has committed the unforgivable sin! No longer will he be permitted aboard this vessel! Nor..." added the irate Feline. "Will the Universal Council Overseer, Clio, father of Bom, be allowed entry! They both are to be blocked, should they wish access by physical means, or teleport in."

Nods of approval, and murmurs of assent followed these words.

"The Universal Council still sits, with that Dog commanding, but...it is divided! Many other races are displeased at the actions of Clio's peoples, knowing full well, he is instigator behind it. But, being of lesser strength, and fearing the Roog might also turn on them, they are unwilling to commit to either side.

"The Feline will no longer be a part of this body! We will not take the murder of our citizens lying down!"

Low growls of resentment filled the room.

"As I said before; Kei appointed a new leader..."

Expectantly, those listening thought Dia referred to herself, but with her next words, the mood in the room exploded.

"Bom not only stole from us my Noor children, among them was their Ultimate Queen, and...it is that female, who is also our revered, appointed head."

Screams of indignation filled the room, as the full implication impacted upon her audience. Warriors rose to their feet, ready to tear the enemy limb from limb. The claws of the male guardians slid out, then in, as if seeking someone, or something on which to vent their rising ire, to avenge the wrong done to the Feline nation.

But, Bom was far away, where none could reach him.

Dia growled a command for silence. Calm slowly returned, but from this point on, the underlying animosity toward the Roog/Feline, Bom, would always be present in the breasts of her crew.

"Until we find our Queen and her Healer Nest, we will proceed thus: I am taking this med ship to the thick of the battle, where the Roog originate; the Forbidden Sector. That is the most likely place for Bom to take his captives. I'm certain by now, there isn't a being aboard this ship, who doesn't know, the prison in the bowels of the Forbidden Planet, is not what it appears to be. He will take her there! Are there any who wish to be excused from this exercise?"

"We are not cowards!" screamed one from the crowd.

"We follow; are loyal to your leadership!" cried another.

"Yet..." Dia returned quietly. "Are we not physicians?"

A murmur of consternation passed through the group.

"So," Dia declared. "This is what we will do. Our warriors will be on constant alert. They are the ship's protection, and should we need to do battle, it is they who will lose their lives.

"We will still serve as a med ship, with the neutrality that goes with it. We the physicians will heal as before, at the forefront of the battle for our Nation and our Queen, tending the casualties among our troops, yet, all the while, like a spy, we will search their installations from a distance, for the ones stolen from us.

"In his establishment, Bom will think he will get the last word, but two can play his game. Covert warriors can enter, and take what is rightful ours. He thinks to hold our Queen, as a means of bargaining for his own amnesty in the end, but we will find her, free her...and when she is returned to us...we will protect her, and her Noor clan at all costs!

"And in the end, for his trouble, Bom, will receive no clemency from us!"

Chapter 4

By now, Bom had realized one important thing: if he was to gain the upper hand, the way to conquer the Junction pair, and their female, was to first eliminate the mental male, for the Roog-half believed, that individual kept the other two protected. And so to that end, Bom first revived Liam.

Oh, I'll not let him come around fully. He's much too dangerous for that.

Entering the storage space, behind the revolving wall, of the larger torture chamber, the Roog/Feline turned the light up...but only to dim.

Anything higher will be suicide.

Imprisoned in a drain belt, and confined in straps against the metal partition, the buff naked Noor took time to open his eyes. Then before Liam could fully comprehend his surroundings, Bom went at him, with repeated, rapid-fire strokes, from the slicing laser weapon in his paw.

Liam made no effort to defend himself; at his low energy level, he was unable. By the time Bom had finished, the Mental male, succumbing to the constant brutal blows, was again unconscious. He now looked more like a piece of tenderized meat, than anything resembling a living creature.

Bom chuckled, delighted by his accomplishment, and turned the dial on the light. As he moved back into the hall, Bom felt proud of himself.

Well, Liam. Let's see you recover from that whipping. You sure won't be much help to the other two now.

****

This time Bom stepped into the main torture chamber, turning the dimmer knob of the light to low as he came in.

On the floor at his feet, lay the chained Noor female. He had wrapped her hands and feet with chain, and by another length, and a metal collar, fastened her to a post in the floor.

Bom had stripped her naked, removed her silver headband, and fancy butterfly earrings. Her short curly white hair wrapped around human-like ears; her face was humanoid, and so was most of her body, but along her back, from neck to waist, was a fine white fur, while protruding from the buttocks was a cat-like tail.

What bothered Bom most was the tiny, barely visible butterfly-shaped wings, just behind her shoulder blades. He had no idea what they were for; no other Noor he knew had them.

Every being that sees you, thinks you are so beautiful. But to me, you are in the likeness of a human animal, merely a cow to be bred or eaten, even if you have a cat tail to go with it. Ugly!

Bom looked to the barred cage across the room. Inside was the one he hated most; Loki! That Noor Physical had so often gotten the upper hand, bested him on more than one occasion.

Why should he always be the favored? I am half, also; no different than he. Yet, Dia blesses him with her constant love, while I am merely tolerated, by her, and...my father.

Bom had deliberately squeezed the heavier Noor into a cage too small for his size. He knew Loki feared being enclosed in a confining space, especially if he could not break loose.

At the moment, the Physical Healer looked like a cream pastry exploding over the sides of its wrapper; his red-blond topnotch hiding his ears; the fine back fur, stark against the white of his naked skin; the tail, lying limp and useless, through the bars.

Where is your strength now, mighty Noor?

Bom laughed, and toned down the lights a smidgeon, just to be safe; in case the Noor's physical strength might be more than bargained on.

The powerful male opened his eyes, and seeing what was before him, began to struggle with the chains that bound his hands and feet together, but the drain-belt at his waist prevented his gaining enough energy. And, Bom had made fast the cage door with another chain and padlock.

No way can you get loose, Noor! For once you are truly helpless.

Bom turned to his shelf of implements; chose a heavy iron bar. The female, though in a drain-belt, was just beginning to stir.

Better be quick, before those hidden powers thwart me.

Bom raised the truncheon above his head; brought it down with all the force he could muster. The blow landed just where he wanted it; right between the eyes of the hapless female. The second blow, meant to cripple, caught the small figure across the right arm and wing.

I know how to punish a wayward cow! I know how to kill one, too! But you need to suffer...long, and painfully...so you'll remember me, and cower before me, when I rule in my father's place.

The blows fell heavily, rapid and no longer with direction, as anger ruled the frustrated attacker. Vengeance was his, and though Clio had ordered the Noor peoples immobilized, yet left functioning, Bom wanted revenge against those he blamed for his lack of recognition.

Behind him, Loki screamed with rage, at his inability to defend his mate; rattled and rocked his confining cage, but all to no avail. And, at the back of the revolving wall, the Mental male was oblivious to it all, unable to help either.

At last, spent by his exertions, Bom stepped back, panting. The bloody bar was cast aside. Satisfied, he had done enough damage here, he turned to leave. Purposely, Bom left the light on dim, so Loki might have a view of the critical female body on the floor.

That's what you get, Noor, for taking what was rightfully my property. The butterfly tattoo on her hand marks her as mine!

Then, Bom went to deal with those that called themselves family, to these he despised.

First, I will incapacitate the males, as I did Liam; that way the females are unprotected. Next will come the older females. That Twila will be a pleasure to cut. And, the two human younger Noor, I will deal with last.

****

Alone in the semi darkness, Loki watch anxiously for some sign of life in his beloved treasure.

Where is Tilk? Why doesn't she come out and protect them? Did that first blow, between the eyes, prevent her? Is the essence finally dead?

But then, Loki remembered:

If it were so, then both would be dead.

And so, he watched expectantly, all through the long hours. At times, he struggled uselessly against his chains, in hopes of freeing himself, so he could go to her.

Finally, confidence faded; hope turned to despair; and an overwhelming fear took its place.

There has been no movement for more than a day.

Where are you Liam? Liam, I need your help. Help me, Mental! Are you dead, too? Oh, please; please...someone...help...me...

As the days passed, Loki at last gave up; his mind went to drifting in and out of madness.

Chapter 5

It had been a living nightmare. Her brother Tommy had come out of the master bedroom about the same time as Tia had met her giant attacker. Tomekichi, too, had been confronted by a second Roog.

But, unlike Tia, who had simply been forced along unresisting, her brother chose to fight for his family. Tia wasn't able to watch, but she heard the unequal battle as it raged behind her, while she descended the stairs to the lower level.

Downstairs, she was herded together with her grandmother, aunt, and aged parents, guarded already by other enormous dogs. Father seemed in a state of shocked compliance, his eyes distant and unseeing, as if he were reliving a reoccurrence of a long ago memory.

Tia quickly realized, her father couldn't tell the present reality from the past experience, when Manzo, as a boy, had been herded with his mother into the barbed wire enclosed compound to await shipment back to Japan.

Soon, sister-in-law, Joy, joined them.

Out on the street, the Roog forced the Japanese family into the back of a semi, to wait with other captured humans. A half hour later, the huge beasts began tossing the bodies of the dead and dying into the vehicle, at the feet of the prisoners. Tomekichi, who mercifully had already passed into the land of his ancestors, was among them.

When the back door of the trailer was lowered, the truck began to move. Tia felt no movement, and she never understood, how one minute they were on the surface, and the next, beneath the ground.

A short time later, the back door was again raised; the prisoners herded along a dimly lit underground passage, where they were forced into filthy cages; crammed together inside them, like cattle.

A Roog stood guard by each cage, but the cross sliding gates were left open. Most inside, had already realized, it was pointless to try to flee.

Next, the men were separated from the women, and led away. Father obeyed, like a compliant animal about to be slaughtered, the women, he was meant to protect, forgotten.

Tia knew, they would never see him again in this life. It was now up to her to see to the welfare of her grandmother, aunt, mother, and sister-in-law.

****

More had been in captivity since he had first sprung up as a shoot, in the wrong place. How his seed pod had come to be at the entrance to the underground prison, will never be known, but with the moisture from the sea covering the rocks around where he grew, he was nourished, until he stood six inches tall; large enough to be noticed.

As a Roog mounted the path from the crashing shore below, on his way to work in the tunnels being constructed, he passed by the struggling sapling, stopped, and insulted that anything living should succeed, pulled the Root being from his crack between the rocks.

More thought his life was at an end. He knew nothing of the silent tree forms, that covered the upper crust above, to which he bore such a resemblance; nor was he aware, that unlike them, he could reason and talk, and belonged to an intelligent species from the stars.

The next morning, when the same Roog passed the spot, and found what he had uprooted was still thriving, out of curiosity, he picked it up, carried it with him into his sleeping cubicle, and stood it in the corner.

Forgotten, More listened, as visitors spent time with his Roog. At first, their conversation seemed nothing but growls, and a constant stream of varying tonal barks, but soon they began to make sense to the young Root.

At one point, one of the visitors, disgusted that his cup only held water, tossed the contents in More's direction. Some landed on the Tree Being, pleasantly soaking him.

The first word that ever came out of the mouth of the small twig in the corner, was 'more'. It not only shocked, and amazed, the giant Roog around the table, it became his moniker.

More did not stay small; he grew to over six feet tall, until presently his form resembled that of a well seasoned redwood, twisted from labor not meant for one of his kind, his dark bark aged, and scarred, but the brain still sharp, intelligent, and knowledgeable.

More found he could pick up languages, though human always seemed to have too many dialects. As with his Roog companions, the Root found he needed a translator to understand it.

He also discovered he had a seer sense. It came and went; he would experience visions, both of the past, and future events to come. These latter, he kept to himself.

Some time in his junior years, More was given a specific duty: to organize, and man the supply depot, and communal grocery. Here he found his calling. It was a place of safety; he could observe without being harassed; here he could learn, and influence the course of the establishment. More was both proud of his enterprise, and devoted to the secret thwarting of his captors' plans.

In his long lifetime, More had seen many species come and go: the Roog, of course. were always present; Felines were their hated enemies, inflicted, when captured, with a horrific torture for the dogs' pleasure. And more recently, More had come in contact with another Root, Zaba, from whom he learn his ancestral tongue, about his culture, and where he originated.

But it was with humans, More felt the most empathy. The mighty warden, Bom, had built his establishment around a breeding, cattle-farm sideline; its real objective. The humans he brought in were his livestock; subjected to appalling conditions, tortured, butchered; all eaten in the end. Most never gained their freedom, and covertly, More devoted his life to making their lives somewhat tolerable, yet for the benefit of their mutual jailors, he feigned dislike of humans.

When the great Noor Healer was brought in as a prisoner, More found another was likeminded, and formed an immediate bond with him. When Loki nearly died by Bom's hand, for some reason, known only to himself, More felt responsible; when the Noor bested Bom, More was elated.

But much had happened since that day. Bom had finally been forced to shut down his human breeding kennels. The Roog/Feline had ordered his Roog cousins to seek their meat up on the surface, and most of the dogs had vacated the premises.

More, left to his own resources, was hesitant to go above, where he had never been. That is, until this day...

Mayhem reigned in the granite halls once again. It seemed, a few disobedient dogs had decided to start up their own cattle enterprise.

When Bom discovered this, More wondered what his reaction would be.

Chapter 6

Tia, huddled together with her female relatives, didn't notice the old woman, as she inched her way toward them using the bars as support, until she spoke from beside them.

"I know a way out of here; but I'll need your help. I can't walk alone; you'll have to support me."

Stunned, Tia turned, to find the crazy old lady, Pam, from the bus shelter.

"You do want to escape, don't you?" Pam demanded.

Her voice was a grating high-pitched whine, that set Tia to shivering with dread.

"Shush! They'll hear you," she cautioned. "You'll draw attention to us, and get us all killed."

"Ha!" Pam laughed. "Shows what you know. Most Roog don't understand a word of human. They need those translators around their throats to communicate with us, and if we are not wearing one, what we say is gibberish to them."

Can it be possible this old woman isn't so crazy after all?

****

They hunkered down, squatting in a back corner, the offensive white senior with them. Tia was expecting the dog guard to react to the strident tones of the woman; Pam was waiting for her answer.

When nothing happened, Tia began to believe the woman had spoken the truth: to the Roog their words were like the barking of a dog to human ears, unintelligible.

"Well..." Pam demanded. "You going to help me out?"

"I need to talk to my family," Tia said to stall, then switched to Japanese.

She presented the case to her elders; they in turn, argued the pros and cons of following the uncertain claims of the Caucasian, and at last came to an agreement.

After a time, Pam declared impatiently: "Man! You guys sure sound like a bunch of oinking pigs."

And you sound like a screeching fowl.

Tia thought this, but did not dare react aloud, to the insult that had been slapped in the face of her family. She knew everyone of her relatives had understood the callous remark, for suddenly, they were very, very quiet. None offered further words of advice.

"Well? Are you game or not?"

Tia looked to her mother. Mother deferred to grandmother. Together, they both nodded. And Tia passed the verdict.

"Yes."

"Okay, then," Pam agreed. "Help me get up. I'll need your support."

With difficulty, Tia pulled the old woman to her feet. Her relatives following, the pair inched along the outer edge of the crowd, then to the corner of the bars, where the Roog stood guard. Here Pam stopped, and quietly waited just behind him.

The big dog had gotten tired of standing, had lowered to his haunches, so that his head and neck were on a level with the humans standing in the cell. His back was to them, and he appeared to be dozing.

Suddenly, Pam's hand flashed out through the bars, caught the band about the creature's throat, and pulled.

Frightened by the action, expecting a reprisal, Tia quickly stepped back. Pam was forced to come with her, which proved to be to their advantage. Unintentionally, the rest of the women in the cell forged forward, effectively hiding the Japanese family, and the foolish white woman.

The giant Roog rose up to his full height, growling, but with his translator gone, the barks that followed were meaningless. He ranted, clearly angry and seeking someone to punish, raved at them ineffectively, until a second guard appeared on the scene.

"What are you so over heated about?"

Incomprehensible, irate barks of explanation issued from the other.

"Oh, is that all. Who cares if they understand you? Let it go. You can get another later."

As the other left him, still obviously discontent, their guard returned to his post, but this time he remained standing, facing his would be tormentors. Understandable fear was apparent in all the women, and he played upon it, growling every now and then to keep them on edge. Eventually, things settled down again.

Pam pulled Tia to the floor. The Japanese women squatted beside her. It was then they noticed what she had stolen: a wide band of some bendable metallic fabric with a dollar-sized button on the end of it. This Pam proceeded to fasten about her neck, with the push switch facing front, in the middle of her throat.

She pressed the small button in, then spoke. What came out was a series of sharp barks, but all humans also heard the words clearly in their own tongue.

"Bom has entered the compound! Run! Flee! He looks for a scapegoat!"

To the amazement of all present, the Roog guards exploded into a frenzy, their sentry rapidly leaving his post in panic.

Pam laughed, and pressed the button again to shut the instrument off.

"Thought that would get them; they're doing this without his knowledge. Well," she added to the crowd around her. "Now's your chance. All you have to do is walk out of here."

****

37

Most of the women had left the cell, scattering in all directions, but Tia and her family remained behind waiting.

"You said you knew a way out," Tia challenged. "How about showing us? Or was that all talk?"

"Well...I don't exactly know where it is, but Bom has a personal transporter pad..."

"Transporter?"

"Yeah. It's a machine that can send you from one place to another in seconds..."

"You're kidding? There really is such a thing? They are that advanced?"

Pam chuckled. "Well, I think mostly they steal technology, but yeah; how do you think they got the truck down here?"

Tia shook her head.

It's plausible, but humans are just beginning such experiments. Man! And they have it!

"Can it get us all out of here?"

Pam shrugged. "If we can operate it."

Tia wasn't worried about that; she felt she could figure it out when the time came.

"So, okay. What do we do now?"

"I guess, we go look for it, and hope the dogs don't catch us again. Help me up here, will you?"

Chapter 7

As he left the second chamber, where the younger Noor were incarcerated, Bom was pleased at his success in brutalizing the rest of his prisoners.

Never again will any of you brave defying me. I have shown you each the power of my laser wand. Liam and the other males have kept the young and the females protected, but now, you all know, what it feels like to be cut!

And Twila, my beautiful arrogant half Feline, you will not reject my advances the next time I make them. Loki will never take the punishment for you again, nor will he be there to defend you. Too bad you are too damaged for me to take you by force right now.

It will be weeks before any of the Noor recover; if they ever do. I can come back later and check, or leave them...nothing more to do here.

Bom was famished! He needed to feed after all that work! But the kitchen of the moon base had long since been shut down; the machinery used to make incalculable battle transports, silent; the personnel having all gone away with the fleet.

Maybe there will still be a human running around loose in the underground cattle pens of the Forbidden Planet. Time to get lunch!

****

The Roog had gotten over their scare, had realized it had been a hoax. They were quickly rounding up the hapless human females, and forcing them back into the cages. This time, they made certain the gate was closed when they left.

It was this scene, that greeted Bom, as he strolled down the hall.

Irate, and taken aback, Bom stopped short.

"What is this?" he bellowed. "Didn't I tell you not to store food! To hunt up on the surface. We no longer keep a herd down here; are not breeding! Get these creatures out of here! If they do not disappear shortly, you will all pay with your lives!"

****

The five Japanese women, and Pam, were in a side tunnel, when Bom's thunderous tones split the air. As he came into view at the junction of two paths, it appeared they were reasonably safe, invisible to the tyrant. His attention was upon his wayward pack. Yet the Asian women behind Tia and Pam whimpered, and slowly slunk away, mother helping grandmother; sister-in-law, the elder aunt.

Tia, riveted to the spot, could only see a side view of the monster, who clearly was leader of these beasts, yet he resembled none of those they'd seen thus far. He literally towered above all others, at least eight feet tall, and he seemed more mangy feline than canine. Bom had the droopy ears, snarling face and slathering, bared teeth of a bulldog; the head dark with tan muzzle, but it was set on the body of a long haired shaggy black cat. It had a bushy tail, tan feet and paws, the claws of which kept extending in and out, viciously.

To add to this formidable picture, his fur was covered in spatters of wet blood, as if he'd just come from a slaughter house after butchering cows.

Tia trembled visibly, wanting desperately to flee, as had the rest of her family, but though she tried to force her back, Pam would not budge. It was as if she'd been waiting for this encounter. And Tia could not in good face, abandon her, when she couldn't walk on her own.

****

A short way behind the two humans, More stood in the doorway of his store, beside himself over all the goings on. He hated confrontation.

Can't stay here any longer. Must leave this place! Not safe here anymore.

Shuddering, he stepped back into his establishment, and turning about, tried to decide what to do. He moaned aloud in consternation at what met his eyes.

Another problem!

From his extra height, he could clearly see, that while his attention had been elsewhere, four human females had slipped in behind him. They were crouched down next to a barrel of cast-off clothing, shivering with fear, thinking he wouldn't see them.

For a moment, More felt compassion for them, but his own fear quickly overrode.

"Out of here! I don't need this now!" he rumbled. It came out of the throat translator in their Japanese tongue. "Go! Go! Use the back way." He pointed off behind them. "There are other ways out of here. I can't be seeing to you this day."

Obediently, they scurried away, and when they were gone, he almost felt guilty for not helping them. More knew it was unlikely they would find one of the few escape routes: the one through the caves to the rocky river shore was alive with Roog; if they found the one above the kitchen, they would die while traveling through it, without guide, or food and water.

It would have been better to have killed them outright. They have the death sentence on them, but then...so do I, if I do not leave this place immediately.

Pam was fed up with this life of pain and suffering.

If it has to come to an end, what better way, than at the hand of the beast who captured me so long ago? But...first I'll bargain with this so called intelligent animal.

Pam pressed the translator button.

"Hey, Bom!" she shouted to get his attention. "Remember me? We made a deal. When you tagged me, and sent me above to spy for you, you said I'd be safe; I'd never have to come down here again."

Bom turned toward her; she had his attention.

"I even gave you something special, not too long ago. Remember, Red Toes? It was me that sent her to you..."

Bom began a low ominous growl from deep within his chest. He turned into their tunnel.

Beside Pam, the skinny Japanese went to shaking so badly, it nearly made them fall.

"Get it together," Pam hissed to Tia. "He's not going to hurt us. If you run, he will hunt you 'till he catches you."

Then readdressing Bom, Pam continued her negotiation.

****

Tia knew it was already too late. Her mouth was dry, heart racing, body trembling so severely from her terror, she felt as if her limbs were about to give way. She wished with all her being, she had never given aid to this treacherous woman.

In a crouch, Bom slowly inched forward, stalking like a panther about to jump upon his prey.

"We have history together," Pam declared. "You owe me!"

Bom snarled maliciously. Apparently, he didn't feel the same.

What is she doing? Does she have a death wish?
Bom was now right beside them.
At least, mother and the others are safe.
But Pam just went on talking.

"I'm old meat, Bom. I know you like them young." A hoarse laugh escaped her throat. "You'd have to be famished to want an old cow like me."

Oh, she's mad! Has she no fear?
For the first time the beast beside them spoke.

"No one bests me and lives, female," he growled. "The one you gave me brought no end of misery, but I have dealt appropriately with her. Now, it is time to give you what you deserve!"

"Oh, but wouldn't you like one more succulent?"

"At this moment, I am extremely hungry..." hissed Bom in a low ominous tone, his face close above them, the slathering mouth dripping.

"How about this one beside me?" Pam suggested calmly.

Tia squealed involuntarily, and slipped from beneath the traitorous white woman's arm, preparing to flee. In one swift motion, the giant Roog had caught Pam by the throat.

Before he straightened, and Tia could even move, Bom's other hand-like paw had grabbed her by the neck, as well.

****

More had seen it all, and knew there was no helping either female. In his opinion, the one called Pam, deserved what she was getting. To provoke this warden was pure suicide. But the other, seemed a victim of circumstance. He pitied her.

Yet More also realized, this was his chance. Bom would head to his quarters, where his personal teleport pad was situated. If he did not stay in the compound, then he would at least jump to a place more private.

And so, as Bom strode by, More stepped back into shadow, and waited. Quietly, he followed after, at a distance, once the inattentive half breed had passed. Bom was too distracted to notice the Root behind him, and as More had hoped led him right to the teleport pad.

More's hope was to witness how the thing worked, but Bom simply stepped up on the platform, and he and his two victims disappeared.

Apparently, it's set to return to the last jump site. Perhaps, I can do the same? But I'll give him a little time to leave, and be feasting elsewhere. Then, I'll follow.

****

Bom had no patience to wait to feed; as he sped down a side corridor of the moon base, he bit the hand from the old one, and swallowed it whole. And all the while, the offensive creature screamed obscenities at him.

Enough of this! I like my meat to fear, and plead in fright, but this one annoys me.

When he reached a vacant room, Bom dropped the skinner captive, so he could use both paws to kill, and tear, at his tough meat. Ignoring his escaping second catch, he scarcely noticed, as she carefully backed from the room.

Distantly, Bom resolved to catch her later.

Chapter 8

The world as they had come to know it since escaping Earth had ceased to exist. With the core Noor family gone, Dia and Kimon were at a loss, seemingly beside themselves. They seldom frequented the home bed nest.

Dia prowled constantly, while her mate worked himself to exhaustion, and slept only when he dropped, which was usually somewhere on a bed in med bay.

Dia's mournful howls could be heard echoing throughout the ship. It was rumored among the males who had known her for near on ninety years, that she was with kit. But most disproved such a fact, for it was well known, Kimon was incapable. The story was, he had been castrated in Bom's prison a long time ago. But what these guardians were not privy to, and the small handful of humans and their mates from her nest were, was that: Tilk/Susa, the Noor Queen, had restored him to male hood with a simple touch. And so, it was quite possible the owner of this ship was carrying.

But if this was so, the small ones inside Dia could not be faring so well. The mother was too often distraught.

The remaining males from her nest, two Feline and one human, were constantly on edge also, keeping their partners close by, as if they feared they too would be snatched. The couples were seldom seen apart; often found in a group. If they became hungry, Thor would accompany Reva to the kitchen to get it. The large elder Feline stood guard, while his human mate prepared a simple fare.

Back at the computer terminals, or boards, as they were known in the Feline tongue, Steven watched the screens for Thor, keeping Amara nearby. Dia normally pleasured in watching the human pair's daughter, TaTa, but because the Feline was so often disconnected, the baby usually played or slept near at hand.

Only the younger Feline, Uel, and his human mate, Feather, dared chance working apart, preferring a semblance of order. The two could be found most often on the med bay floor, tending to wounded casualties. Feather would be found seated on a stool, bandaging a wounded limb, with Uel possessively close at hand.

Often, the patient the human woman was tending, would reach out to her extended belly, as if to be reassured the life inside was real. At that point, a growl of warning from Uel would cause the paw to be immediately withdrawn.

The ship that housed them was now in the allotted sector of the Roog, in the thick of the most active battle zone in the universe. They were positioned at the entrance to the solar system, behind the outer most planet, and the Forbidden World, the third from the sun, was in full view on every one of Thor's screens. He had been monitoring, searching since their arrival, for some sign of a Noor gleam.

Dia stepped into the cubicle. It seemed one of her better days. She was lucid, almost calm for a change.

"Find anything yet?" she asked.

Thor glanced up from his board, and shook his large head.

"I've covered every square inch inside the planet and on the surface with the deepest probe available," he admitted discouraged. "If they are alive, they are either not there, or not alive."

"I refuse to believe they are dead." Dia sighed. "Where else could he have taken them? That planet is the only place he has ever considered home."

Uel hissed an unpleasant word beneath his breath, disagreeing heartily with the prison being assessed as a home, for he too had unwillingly grown up in its confines. After a moment's deliberation, he came up with a thought.

"Sometimes, Bom would leave the underground complex," he revealed. "I don't think he would go far. When he went, he would use his own teleport pad for a short distance. He was never gone for long, so he didn't come here, or to any other solar system. He just wanted to eat alone undisturbed. He may have some other post set up on one of the uninhabited planets nearby."

The human, Steven, broke in with a suggestion. " I could take a shuttle and search among the other worlds. The battle rages beyond us, and I think I could get away undetected."

Thoughtfully, Dia nodded.

"Okay. But you will not go alone. All three of you go, or none go at all, and...your females remain here safe with us."

Each of the males frowned, reluctant to be parted from their partners.

"What if Feather should go into labor?" Uel asked tentatively. "The little one might come early?"

"We will take care of her," Dia reassured softly. "Do you think I have never assisted at a human birth before?"

"I will miss the coming of my small one," objected Uel.

Dia hissed. "It is the product of rape," she stated bluntly. "Not yours!"

And daringly, Uel defied her.

"Mine!" he growled. "And always will be. I chose this human female. Her offspring will be my treasure, no matter how it was conceived."

"Good!" declared Dia. "So, you have a reason to come back. Now, trust me to take care of them both."

"You will not kill it?"

"Have I ever killed a new born? How many of the Noor young were in my hands? I did not destroy them, though there was a decree to do so."

"Sorry." Uel dropped his head in submission, and said no more.

"Forgotten." Dia returned to the matter at hand. "You pilot the shuttle, Thor. If you come under fire, any of our battleships will assist you. I doubt there is any warrior, aboard any Feline manned vessel, who does not now know whom we seek. The whole Universe awaits the finding of our Queen. Don't come back without them!"

Chapter 9

To the accompaniment of receding horrific shrieks, Tia fled in heart hammering panic. Through half lit underground tunnels of obsidian stone, terrified for her life, she searched frantically for a place to hide from her giant beast captor.

At last, when her legs would no longer carry her, the Japanese girl came upon an unlit side tunnel, which led to a dead end, and a very small dark room, filled with abandoned crates. Panting with exhaustion, gasping for breath, Tia crawled as far back as she could get, behind the farthermost crate.

Settling down against the ice-cold wall, her mind at last slowed, and she was able to assess her predicament.

If I could just get back to that transporter pad...but, no! That's the first place he'll think I'll go.

Yet, maybe later on...if I could? I could see if I could operate the console, change the destination, and get out of here. Anywhere else is preferable to this!

Listening intently for sounds of pursuit, Tia thought she heard movement at the other end of the room, by the doorway she had entered.

Oh, what if he can track me by scent? What if he can follow where I've gone? What if he got ahead of me, and he's already in this room with me?

I'm surely going to die!

****

When he moved his head, Tza saw the human slink into the room, but by this time he was too dehydrated and malnourished to care; all hope had fled.

He watched her hide, saw clearly in the darkened room where she was, but only with a listless half interest.

Another of Bom's victims. Supper got away, did it Bom? Well, he'll catch it soon.

Or am I just hallucinating? Am I that hungry? I'd never consider eating a human, as that dog does.

Death must be close...be merciful when it comes...

****

Tia must have dozed off. She jerked awake. From off in the distance she could hear her stalker, but he wasn't being stealthy. Bom was striding with purpose.

Oh, gosh! He knows where I am! I'm next on the menu.

Trying to appear smaller, to vanish if she could, Tia crawled into the empty crate beside her. She knew the action could trap her, yet she hoped with his size, he wouldn't see her as soon.

If I just keep very quiet...

Slowing her breathing, Tia waited for the inevitable.

****

Bom entered the room, flipped on the light switch. Though the illumination was dim, and only at this end, it was right over Tza. Bom knew it would temporarily blind the small Feline, but that's the way the Roog-half wanted it.

The sadistic warden waited until he saw the fettered young male's eyes focus on him.

"Want some lunch, Tza?" Bom barked out a humorless laugh, as he held up the remaining leg of his human catch. "Actually, I brought you a whole one, but the stupid, skinny human got away from me. I killed this one though; she provoked me to no end."

As Tzachok gave no reaction, Bom continued to taunt. "Not hungry enough yet? Oh, I forgot. Pure Feline are particular; they don't like human meat. Too bad."

Tza daringly hissed a Feline swear under his breath.

"What's that, small one?" Bom sneered. "I think your translator got turned off when I bound you. Here let me fix that. I'd like to hear what you have to say in the Roog tongue...if you dare."

Bom dropped to one knee, casting aside for the moment the remains of his meal. He reached over and punched the button at his prisoner's throat.

"There, that should help." He then stood up to his full height, towering over his unfortunate helpless prisoner. "I'll just leave you this leg, in case you get hungry enough. It's tough, old meat; not real tasty, unless you are famished like I was from my work. I would have preferred that younger one, but she slipped down a tunnel, and I lost her scent. Too clean. You haven't seen a human she, have you?"

"Do you think I would tell you if I had?" Tza retorted bravely.

Bom chuckled, delighted at the rise he had gotten.

"Oh, well. I take it you don't want this, then." Bom picked up the uneaten morsel, and tauntingly took another bite. "Just wanted to tell you, I'll be heading out now. My work for the moment is done here. Don't know if there will be reason to come back for a month or two. I might come see if my Noor friends are still alive. But as for you...and your escaped lunch...you should have perished by then...unless of course, you can get free, and catch her."

"And how do you expect me to do that?"

"Oh, did I forget to tell you? I left a small pen knife in the corner by the entry." He barked an unpleasant laugh, amused by his own joke. "But then, you can't get to it all tethered to the wall, can you?"

Tza finally whimpered acknowledgement of his plight.

"Well, just in case you think you can get off this moon by the telipad, I intend to disable it at this end, and set it to self-destruct just after I make my jump. Have a slow, unpleasant death, little helper. To your credit, you were an asset to me, an obedient mechanical."

As he vacated the room, Bom could hear the despairing, plaintive moans of his captive behind him. And as all bullies, he took pleasure in the sounds.

Oh, how I relish the conquer of the weaker ones!

****

Through the slats of the crate, Tia had watched the whole encounter. And once Bom had turned on Tza's translator, she could understand both sides of the conversation, though instead of hearing the language of dog talk, she heard everything in her own tongue.

Even after Bom, on his way out, flipped the light switch off; for a time, Tia could still make out a faint image of the beautiful, man-sized white cat, against the dark wall behind him, as he lay there bound by the dirty ropes. After that vision faded, except when he blinked or closed them, she could see his eyes shining blue-white out of the darkness.

She waited until Tza, the cat, seemed to sleep, and the silence told her, Bom was no longer a threat. Then, she crept cautiously forward from her corner, inch by inch, slowly, to the doorway, and began searching, by feel with her hands, round and round, for the knife that had been mentioned.

Tza did not stir, appeared to hear nothing. He seemed to have given in to his despondency.

****

In the misery of his plight, Tza had forgotten the presence of the hidden human at the back of his prison. It wasn't until he felt her cold hands against his fur, that he opened his eyes in shocked amazement.

Up close, her skin was a smooth golden brown. The long black straight hair fell across her shoulders, and had an almost maroon tint to it. Her brown eyes were narrowed, as she concentrated on sawing at the rope about his neck. Shivering, as if in fear, or from the frigid air about them, small impatient puffs of steam vapor escaped her lips. Her fragrance was not unpleasant.

Is she trying to set me free? Why would she do that?

Chapter 10

Bom had just finished setting the console to self-destruct after his next jump transfer. He turned around to step to the teleport pad, but was shocked to find he was not alone. The Root from the prison supply store was standing big as life before him. The tree-being appeared equally surprised to see him.

"What are you doing here, you stupid Root?" Bom demanded incensed. "Did you follow me?"

More seemed speechless, which annoyed Bom all the more.

I do not have time for this! I have only minutes to get out of here.

"Well, have it your own way! Your stupidity will cost you your life this time. Enjoy spending your last hour in this cold rock. Remember, it was your choice."

With that Bom stepped around him, mounted the port pad, and teleported back to the prison.

****

More had expected the warden to be long gone. He had waited for hours, just to be safe. But when he had materialized, there was Bom right there in front of him, his back turned, working at the controls of the machine.

As More stepped down, Bom turned around.

The Root fully expected to be challenged, to have to fight, but all he'd received was a dressing down. He was used to that; nothing unusual in it. But now that Bom was gone, doubts assailed More.

What did he mean? What is this place? Where am I?

The humming console suddenly change to a high pitched whine, and More realized what the Roog/Feline had been doing.

Time to get out of here! He must have set it to self-destruct.

He stepped to the teleport platform, but nothing happened. More waited. Still nothing.

The Root stepped off again, and went to the vibrating board. He fiddled with the dials, then stepped back on the pad.

And the room exploded in a brilliant flash of light. More never heard the deafening percussion.

****

The white cat-man just lay there, as if he didn't believe he was free. Tia reached out to reassure, to stroke the long fur on his back, but the creature hissed a warning, snarled as if afraid of her, so she sat back on her heels to wait him out.

Maybe, they don't like to be touched?

"I'm not going to hurt you. I'm just trying to help. We're in the same position; we could help each other."

The man sized feline seemed unable to understand, just lay there panting, as if he couldn't get enough air. With the position of the rope about his neck, it had probably long been difficult to breathe.

"I know your name is Tza. I heard that awful beast call you that..."

He finally spoke, his voice gravelly from lack of moisture.

"Tza...me...yes."

"Okay, then. I don't mean you harm."

He shook his head.

"Without translator, I am unable to understand you."

"Oh. You mean, I need one of those things like around your neck?"

She reached out again, to show him she understood, to touch the band he wore, but he misinterpreted the action, and growled at her instead.

****

Tza hadn't meant to show negative reaction. It had been pure reflex, and in his present weakened state, he had little control. His limbs were trembling so badly, he knew he would not even be able to stand. It meant he was helpless, at the mercy of this female, and that fear made him react badly.

She's an unfamiliar. I've been taught since very young, most humans of the forbidden planet are cruel to Feline. They keep them as pets, even sterilize them so they can't breed. Rumors are they do so in the most sadistic ways.

But this she...seems nice. Dare I trust her?

****

At last, he sat up.

"I'm Tia," she stated, pointing to herself.

He nodded, swallowed, spoke with difficulty.

"Need water..."

"Sorry, I have no idea where there is any. I haven't looked in any of the rooms but this one."

When he shook his head again, she remembered he couldn't understand.

Goodness. How are we going to communicate, if he doesn't understand a word I say?

Then Tza shocked her by standing up on his hind limbs like a human.

Whoa! What kind of cat is this?

He stumbled toward the doorway, as if suddenly on a mission, sniffed at the air, then using the wall as support, began following the dark corridor.

Tia followed after, somewhat nervously.

If Bom comes back, and we meet him, we are finished.

****

Once Tza had gained better use of his limbs, and a second wind to give him strength; when he smelled water, he took to all fours, loping through the lighted hallways, soon losing the human.

He turned into a large room, apparently meant to be a kitchen. He could hear the splat of the drops now, smell the odor of stagnant water, and suddenly there across from him was the dripping tap.

Tza tried to turn the small wheel-shaped handle, but it was seized tight, so, desperate for a drink, he dropped to a crouch, and lapped from the puddle on the floor.

Oh...so good. Never knew water could taste so heavenly.

"Tza?"

The she human was calling from not far away, but he was still too thirsty to take time to tell her the way, so he yowled out a mournful note, long and high pitched, to guide her to where he was.

I'm going to have to find that creature a translator.

****

Tia entered the room panting for breath, somewhat annoyed that she'd been left to fend for herself, but when she saw what Tza had found, all was forgotten.

Water! Oh golly; am I ever thirsty!

He was lapping from a puddle on the stone floor.

"Why don't you turn the tap on?" she demanded, grabbing at the turn wheel.

But though she put all her strength behind it, it wouldn't budge.

Well, that explains why he's drinking off the floor.

Tia looked about her: tall table-like counters with odds and ends scattered about. She could just barely see them.

"Tza...Tza! Help me!"

This time she didn't care if he growled at her; she grabbed him by the arm, and pulled at him. And indeed, he did hiss warningly, but by now he was less parched, and finally allowed her to drag him to the nearest counter that held drawers.

Through pantomime, she got him to understand, she wanted him to lift her up. Abruptly, Tza had his arms around her waist, she was rising rapidly into the air, and from that vantage point, she could see above the counter top, and pull out the drawers to search them.

She found all sorts of knives and cleavers; on top, bowls and cups. And...

Is that a pipe wrench?

Tia grabbed up one of the bowls, and the wrench, and signaled down. She ran to the tap, with Tza following. Tia set the bowl at their feet, and began to pound with the wrench to loosen the tap. Tza finally took it from her.

"Me!" he declared.

To her surprise, with finger-like paws, he adjusted the grip on the implement, surrounded the wheel, and with much effort, pulled powerfully against the rusty wheel, until it suddenly moved, and the flow from the tap increased.

"Oh, yes. Oh, yes!" Tia exclaimed in delight.

He dropped the wrench with a clatter, and caught up the bowl from the floor.

Tia craved moisture desperately, but she knew he must be far more dehydrated, for obviously he'd been here much longer. She was prepared to wait.

Yet, when the bowl was filled with water, the Feline turned to her, offering her a drink.

"Females always first," Tza proclaimed, as if he'd been taught chivalry all his life.

Tia chuckled.

What a rare find. How many earthmen would be this gallant?

Chapter 11

After they drank their fill, they searched around the small kitchen, but found nothing edible.

Tza told Tia to wait there for him, and then took off. As soon as he was gone, Tia immediately was fearful. He felt like a protector, even though he wasn't much taller than she; couldn't be more than five foot six at the most; hardly an adversary for one as big as Bom.

****

Tza wanted a translator for the human, and the best place he thought he could find one, would be where Bom had originally brought the two females. The Roog/Feline had mentioned, the one he'd eaten had been most trying to him. Tza also knew Bom so disliked the human tongue, he refused to even try to learn it. Logic told the younger male, the other female must have been wearing a translator to speak with Bom.

Tzachok loped through the tunnels going not by sight, but by the scent of the blood trail, backtracking to the very room where the orgy had begun. When he entered, he almost changed his mind. The sight and odor overwhelmed, so he found himself gagging, and for a moment, he had to hold his breath, so he wouldn't lose the moisture he'd so recently ingested.

Finally, he steeled himself, stepped across the bloody floor to a pile of castoff clothing, and began to search through them. He did not find what he sought.

All about the room were signs of the desperate struggle the unfortunate female had put up: bits of skin, torn and blood crusted; pieces of gouged flesh, chewed, then regurgitated. Tza retched, swallowed to keep his focus. He had to search those remnants.

With great reluctance, he went to the small pile of castoff remains, forced himself with eyes closed, going by feel, to paw through what was there, and was rewarded.

He couldn't leave the room fast enough.

****

It wasn't long, and Tza returned, holding in his hand what looked like a bloody strip of meat.

Tia shivered at the sight.

What did he do? Is he that hungry, that he went to find what was left of Pam?

He went to the tap, and held it under the running water until the object was no longer tinted red. Tza turned off the flow, dried it on his fur, and looked up.

When he approached, Tia stepped back, repulsed, until she realized, what he held out to her, was the translator Pam had stolen from the guard back in the cells.

"Hope this still works," Tza said optimistically. "It's been through...ah...never mind. Put it on. Then we can communicate."

Okay, then. Guess, I don't need to know where it's been.

But she could guess, and that made the very act of putting it around her neck something less than pleasant. Yet after the fact, it didn't matter where the instrument came from; it was a method by which they could understand each other.

Tia made quick work of fastening it about her throat, and pressing the button in to turn it on.

"Does it work? Can you understand me?"

"Aye! Yes! They are made pretty sturdy."

"Now what?" she asked expectantly.

"We must seek the others."

"What others?"

"Bom had me help bring in other...ah...prisoners. I'll not abandon them."

"Okay. But are we safe? Is that beast gone?"

"As far as I can tell, yes."

****

Tza led them through the halls much slower this time. He seemed to know where he was headed. Soon they entered a dimly lit room, with a cage, the size of a small jail cell, back in the shadows.

When Tza turned up the lights, the sight that met their eyes made them both cringe. But the Feline appeared more prepared, and ignoring the battered female at their feet, went directly to the wall behind. Somehow, he made the partition revolve.

Strapped behind the wall was a combination cat/humanoid. He was tall, at least seven feet or more, approximately five hundred pounds. Most of his body was man-like, but from waist to neck on his back, he had short silver fur with light black markings, and just barely visible, in the straight short hair atop his head, were tiny cat-like ears. Almost invisible, between his naked legs was a tail as long as he was tall, and his manhood resembled that of a feline, hidden beneath, inside.

But the most disconcerting thing about this male was his condition. Every inch of the once smooth skin was lacerated, as if it had been cut with a whip; he resembled more raw meat than a breathing person.

"Ah, Poppa," moaned Tza. "What has he done to you?"

"Is he alive?" asked Tia.

"I think we'll have to wait to see," Tza ventured. ""He is Noor. They draw energy from the light source, and now that I've turned it up, maybe...not sure if he's able to store while in that belt."

Tia had noticed the flexible, wide, metallic belt about his waist.

"What is that for?"

"It's meant to keep them weak. But, we'll wait and see. I don't have a key to open and remove it. Maybe, he can come around anyway."

"Is he a criminal?"

"No!" Tza exploded. "The Noor are Healers! Bom simply hates them..."

Tia waited, but Tza didn't elaborate. Finally, he spoke again.

"I know they need water to heal themselves. It's as essential to them as is the light. Stay here with them, and I'll go get a pail of water."

Tia didn't want to remain alone in the room with the dead and dying, but Tza was gone before she could object. She wasn't as superstitious as were many of her people; she had a modern education, but still, it made her nervous at the prospect of being alone with the departed.

While Tza was away, she took the time to examine the other two prisoners. The one crammed in the cage, resembled the creature on the wall, excepted this one was at least fifty pounds heavier, and the fur on his back was auburn; the topnotch of reddish-brown curls. He didn't appear hurt, though he also was fitted with a belt. It seemed impossible, he could be comfortable rammed into a cage at least three sizes too small. His eyes were closed, mouth hung half open, and he was drooling; his face held a strained pain-filled look, like a dumb tortured animal, who had at last given up.

The Japanese woman turned her eyes to the mangled female at her feet. She was similar also, but much smaller, about the same height as Tia, and thin. Her short curly hair, and back fur were silver-white. It appeared she'd been beaten with some sort of bar, for the metal rod was lying nearby.

Tia felt certain, she was dead, but just to make sure, she knelt down for a closer look. Reaching out to turn her over, she gasped, with the sudden pain of the shout, she heard in her head. It was so audible, and excruciating, it stopped her hand in midair.

"Do not touch her!"

Tia wasn't sure if the voice came from the wall or the cage, but she quickly obeyed, sitting back on her heels. She looked around, first at the one on the wall, but he hadn't moved; his head still hung; his chin on his chest. The other in the cage, was also just as he had been.

Maybe I didn't really hear that...imagination getting to me? Or the spirits of the dead talking?

Tia shivered with dread.

****

Tza entered the room, lugging a full pail of water, sloshing it about because the load was too heavy. He knew immediately something was wrong, by the look on the human's face, and the sense of panic that emanated from her like a visible wave.

"What's the matter?" he asked apprehensively. "What happened?"

"Aw...nothing. I thought I heard someone talk to me."

"Was the voice in your mind?"

"Yes! How did you know that?"

Ignoring the question, Tza set the pail of water next to the prisoner against the wall.

"The Noor are telepathic," he stated calmly.

"So...I wasn't imagining it?"

"No. One of them must be awake, even if they don't seem so." He turned his attention to the injured male. "Poppa Liam! Can you hear me?"

****

Why does he keep calling him, poppa?

"Is this man your father?" Tia asked curious.

Tza shook his head. "Why?"

"Well, poppa is a word for father..."

"Oh! No. In the Feline society, Poppa is a title of respect. Liam is a rescuer of many orphans."

"Are you an orphan, then? Did he rescue you?"

"Yes. I was born to slaves on a Roog planet. They tortured my father; killed my mother, shortly after she gave birth and hid me...she named me Tzachok. It means laughter... It gave her a moment of pleasure to have me..."

"The Roog have no mercy. I have seen what they do on my world...we have a common enemy."

Tza decided not to comment on the matter, turned instead to the injured Noor on the wall.

"Poppa! Liam!" he challenged. "Do you hear me?"

Tza took a cloth from the water in the pail, wrung it out, and went to washing the legs of the unresponsive male before him. Suddenly, a voice screamed in both their minds.

"Tza! That is beastly cold! Please, stop it!"

Tza chuckled, stepped back. "At least, it woke you up."

Liam moaned, and spoke aloud.

"Not funny, kit!" After a long pause, he added with effort: "Where is Loki? I feel him but can't at present see..."

"You are blind?" questioned Tza. "Why don't you look by mind?"

"My mental ability is very limited. And physically, I have no vision either. But I feel Loki in the room...where?"

Tza sighed, as if reluctant to disclose what he saw.

"He...is in...a cage."

"Spit!" hissed Liam.

"Poppa!" reproved Tza. "Such language. There is a human female present."

Is that considered a swear in their tongue?

"Aw, Tzachok. Forgive. I have little control in my condition. My apology, female."

"I've heard worse," Tia returned grinning. "And I'd say, you have good cause to say something even more colorful."

"Wait a minute," Liam reasoned. "You said, 'human', Tza? Where are we?"

"On the moon of the Forbidden Planet," answered Tza.

"And how came you to be here?"

"Long story, Poppa. If you cannot read me, I will tell you at a later date. I am much ashamed...of my actions."

"I am certain, anything you did was under duress...nothing to regret."

Once again, Tza left the words go unchallenged.

"Poppa, how do I get you free?"

"First...I want to know of Susa."

"Your female?"

"Yes."

Tza let the silence go on for a moment; finally he dared to answer.

"I think, she is dead, Poppa."

"Not!" disagreed Liam. "We still live. She and we, the Junction, are...as one. I see...deep within her mind...a small evidence of life...both physical and mental. Where is she, male?"

"But," interrupted Tia. "Didn't you tell me not to touch her?"

His response was most unusual. He began to chuckle in delight, from deep down in his chest.

"Loki," he said finally. "He is aware of her. You must have been near her, a threat, so he reacted in the only way he could. That is good! Where is the physical body of my female?"

"At our feet," Tza supplied.

"How badly is she damaged?"

Tza sighed. "Much broken, Poppa."

"Okay. The body can always be repaired. First order of business; you must free Loki."

"Not you, Poppa?"

"Loki is our strength; he is still responsive, or he would not have protected Susa. He can set me free, when he is loose."

"But, how?" whined Tza apprehensively. "I...I..."

Suddenly sensing something vital was undisclosed, suspicious immediately, Liam growled: "You what? Spill it, male!"

"I...put him in there. There is no way...to get free..."

"Why?" asked Liam, his tone dripping of icy, barely controlled anger.

Tza began to shiver with visible fear. Tia also could not understand why he had done such a thing.

"Why?" repeated Liam.

"Master, I have betrayed you. Kill me now."

A long silence followed, broken only by the expectant, terrified gulps from the Feline, Tza.

Liam seemed to be debating his pros and cons. Finally, he spoke again, his tone more conciliatory.

"Tza, sometimes our Maker allows us to get into predicaments...It works in strange ways. No matter why or how you were forced to help confine us, you are also, now, our only salvation. So, pull it together. I cannot at the moment punish you, nor would it accomplish anything. You are not the first to fail us, nor will you be the last to whom we owe forgiveness..."

"But...how do I ever undo what I have done?" groaned Tza. "There is no way to free him."

"To your mind, maybe. You must first find a key to these belts."

Chapter 12

More opened his one remaining eye. The ear near the floor was still functioning also. He could hear voices in the distance, as they echoed off the walls. He could also understand the telepathic projections of the Noor, Liam.

They need a belt key.

For eons the Root had given in to his species' one flaw: the need to gather and store articles of little interest to others. More had kept his stash in a pouch at his waist. As he looked about, he realized his bottom half was no longer a part of him; it had been blown away; lay across the room against the far wall.

He began to howl in abject misery. There was no way he could get to the opposite side of the room.

And I have the key that they seek.

****

Liam stopped short in mid sentence.

"Silence! Listen!"

A mournful, hollow sound filled the caverns, like the blowing of wind through a tube.

"What is that?" whispered Tia apprehensively.

"A Root," Liam supplied. "And I believe he is dying."

Liam went from verbal to mind projection. "Who are you?" he questioned. Then: "Where are you?"

The despondent howl answered each time, then went silent.

"What is a Root?" Tia asked of Tza in an undertone.

"A tree-like being..."

"Be silent!" Liam ordered curtly. "So I can read him."

After many seconds of intense concentration, Liam revealed to them what he had learned.

"It is More, from the planet prison's supply store. He says he has the key we need. Go find him; he is in the transporter room."

Tza rose up obediently.

"You too Tia. Tza will need your help."

****

When they entered the room, it was a shambles. There had been some sort of explosion, and Tia quickly realized, the teleport device would be useless to them.

All about the chamber were bits and pieces of wood and metal. Across the room, in a far corner, lay what appeared to be a blacken block of wood, with an eye painted on it.

"Here," came from the stump, and the eye moved to look at them.

Tia almost screamed aloud from the shock of it.

This is a Root? It's wearing a translator.

Tza hurried over; Tia stayed in the doorway to be safe.

****

As Tza knelt beside the damaged Root, the creature spoke with difficulty.

"I have little time," More stated bluntly. "You cannot help this warrior, but...I will not have died in vain."

"Are you sure there is nothing I can do for you?"

"Only...be with me...when I breathe my last."

"Without question," agreed Tza.

"Across...on the opposite side..."

Tza turned to look in the direction indicated. He recognized the lower half of Root being, and shivered at the implications.

There is indeed no helping this one.

More seemed to read the thought. "Don't waste your time on me," he stated. "When I am gone...beneath the other half, you will find a pouch...around my waist. Inside...is what you seek..."

Tza had no time to mourn this loss, to grieve for the brave old Root, nor to nurse the anger at the injustice of its death, which, he was certain was Bom's handiwork. He watched as More struggled, his mouth gasping at one last breath. A woeful moan escaped the creature, a howl so plaintive, it shook Tza to the core. Then the tree-being lay silent, and still.

****

Tza finally joined Tia.

"It is dead," Tza stated with little evident feeling. "I will need help to lift the other half. The key we seek is in a pouch on that half of the body."

Tia shivered.

How gruesome. We must rob a corpse?

Fear filled her with dread, as she remembered old Japanese superstitions. Tia went to keening in fright. "I will never see my grandfather...my ancestors will never forgive."

"What? What upsets you so?" asked a bewildered Tza.

"If I desecrate a dead body...my ancestors...will not welcome me on the other side..."

"Oh, shush, shush. You are overwrought with all that has happened to you. You are in a new world now. Fallacy cannot follow you here."

The tears came then, and Tza was beside himself to know what to do for her. So, he did the only thing taught to him by nature; he wrapped her in his comforting fury arms, and licked at her tears.

"Shush...shush," he whispered. "Tza will protect you." And again, he licked a tear from her cheek.

Tia suddenly began to giggle uncontrollably.

Tza drew back, puzzled. "What is so funny?"

"I am ticklish..." She closed her eyes so the tears would stop flowing, and tried to calm the crazy laughter. Tza waited patiently; finally spoke.

"You come now?" he ventured hopefully. "The others need us. I have done a bad thing...and must...save face."

That Tia understood, and so she followed.

****

When they returned to the torture chamber, it was as they had left it. The nightmare was still very real.

Liam opened his eyes.

"More is dead?"

"Yes, Poppa," Tza returned sadly. "But, he died a valiant warrior."

Liam accepted with a nod; then abruptly went to the business at hand.

"It will take two of you to open the belt. Go to the back of the cage, behind Loki. You must do it through the bars. He may become violent."

"The transporter is destroyed, Liam," Tza revealed, as the young pair moved to obey. "I don't know how we'll ever get off this rock without it..."

"One problem at a time," the Noor encouraged. "Narrow vision is the best at a time such as this."

Tza stepped to the back of the cage, Tia following. Loki's hips were pressed against the bars, his tail passed through to the outside, limp against the stone floor. The belt back was plainly visible, as was the key hole, and the square pressure points on either side.

"Insert the key, and turn it," instructed Liam. "Then each of you, one on each side, press hard against the pressure points, simultaneously."

When they did as they were told, a resounding click could be clearly heard, resulting in a widening crack which began at the middle of the key hole.

"Now, remove the key. Reach in, and both of you pull a side away from the flesh."

Tia had no idea what to expect, but Tza grit his teeth and steeled himself, knowing what would follow. He had heard this process described by others.

With each clutching a side, they yanked at the same time.

Loki let out a horrific, ear splitting scream, a sound harsh enough to curdle the blood of any warrior used to battle. Tia, unprepared as she was, fainted dead away, at the sight of the large bloody probes that were revealed, as they pulled from the flesh.

Tza needed to be quick. When he pulled her to safety, she was unaware of his ministrations.

Chapter 13

When Tia surfaced to reality, Loki was violently rattling the bars of his cage, a madman in the frenzy of intense pain.

She sat up, dizzy, extremely aware of the frigid air about them. When Tza noticed her shivering, he pulled her onto his lap, and surrounded her with his warm furry arms.

"Feeling better now?" he whispered in her ear.

But her thoughts were only for the poor creature in the cage.

"Why would they put them in such belts?" she asked indignantly. "How cruel. I never thought they'd have things inside, imbedded in the flesh."

"The Roog hate the Noor with a passion. They made the device."

"Just what is it meant to do?"

"Drain their energy..."

"There is one on Liam...and the girl, too."

"Ah huh," agreed Tza.

From the wall, Liam chose to interact with the male in the cage, as he'd finally relaxed in exhaustion.

"Loki..."

"Ah," complained Loki. "I can hear you. No need to thunder in my head."

"Forgive. My control is at a low," apologized Liam. "Can you break free of your chains?"

Loki sighed wearily. "So little light..."

"You need to try...or we'll never be free. " Liam added as incentive. "Susa needs you..."

"No pressure, eh?"

Liam chuckled.

Loki hissed viciously. "I'll kill that beast, when I am free! He made me watch."

"Spit!" Liam swore. But he was ever the voice of reason. "Killing him won't save her..."

"I know that!" growled Loki, and went broodingly silent.

After a time, his muscles began to strain. Long minutes passed as the cords expanded, then contracted, and the process was repeated, over and over. At first, it didn't seem to make much difference; then suddenly, the chains simply fell away.

Tza let out an unrestrained cheer.

"Okay," Liam encouraged. "Next, the cage."

"Give me a moment to catch my breath, will you?" Loki grunted in annoyance. "I'm not a machine, you know."

"Your pain is showing again..."

"I have every right to be growly. It's not just my pain I'm feeling...got yours, and...hers too, to contend with. Maybe, you'd like to be the empath?"

"I would, if I could, Physical."

Loki grunted. "Sorry. Thanks. Didn't mean to be vindictive. I don't think we've ever been this low before...at least not together."

"I hear you...whenever, you are able."

Loki reached out to opposite sides of the barred cage, and began to strain again.

"Why don't you let me find the key to the padlock," suggested Tza.

"Would take too much time," Loki objected. "I'll have it in a minute."

He pushed, and abruptly, all four walls collapsed outward.

"Wow," marveled Tza. "You are strong!"

"It's just a matter of pressure on the right points. The weld was already weak," disagreed Loki. "Been working at that for days..."

"Are you able to stand?" Liam asked. "You've been confined for a long time."

"Don't really care," Loki returned petulantly. "If I have to, I'll crawl. I need to get to Susa."

****

Loki whimpered plaintively, when he touched the mangled heap on the floor. Then he howled long and ominously in anger.

"She's so broken, Liam," he cried out in agony. "I couldn't heal her, even if I was at full power. That beast took a metal bar to her."

"We'll fix her," encouraged Liam. "Don't give up, Loki. I need you to free me now."

Loki seemed to ignore him, intent upon the injured female. Sighing, he ran his hand gently over the shattered shoulders.

"I swear, this is enough to make a Noor hate..."

"Hate would make us no better than he. Please, Loki, set me free."

****

When Liam had sufficiently recovered to stand, he left the room. Loki again crawled to the side of his unconscious mate.

"Where is Liam going?" asked Tza out of curiosity.

"He's looking for something of Susa's he wants back," Loki returned defensively.

Tza suddenly remembered the other prisoners.

"Loki," he ventured. "Bom, took the rest of the family, as well."

"What!" exploded Loki angrily. "He has the children? How did that happen?"

Tza cowed, reluctant to disclose his part in the matter. He was saved by the reentry of Liam.

"Found her headband..." He held up a thin, silver circlet.

"Did you know, he also has the young ones here?" Loki demanded.

"Figured that was so," returned Liam calmly. "There was more than one band in his storage locker."

"How can you be so unconcerned by that?" challenged Loki. "Who knows what he has done to Twila...and the younger females."

"It's done. We can't change it," Liam retorted realistically, squatting beside the female on the floor. "Move aside, so I can get her band on."

"Tilk had no time to enter it, you know..."

Liam looked at Loki questioningly. "Then, where...is she?"

"Maybe, this time we have lost the Essence?" Loki reasoned. He peered intently at his Mental self. "Can you see again?"

"Dimly, but enough." Liam stood to his feet. "Let's get out of here..."

"I'll carry her," Loki agreed. "I noticed you also found the earrings we gave her?"

Tenderly, he lifted the battered woman into his arms, holding her against him like a porcelain doll that would break. He too, rose to full height.

Liam grunted, as if dissatisfied by the situation, and started away. "Come on Tza; show us where the others are."

Chapter 14

The room was like the other, only larger. Around the walls were the males of varying ages, each in the same condition as they had found Liam, and at their feet, the females too were bound to posts by chains, ripped by cuts, bruised by kicks, all naked, in belts, and unconscious. Some appeared more humanoid than others; others were more cat-like, but it was obvious they were all of mixed Noor blood, because the belts had done their work to render them helpless.

There were eight of them: four males; four females. Tia could easily guess who belonged to whom. If you matched the younger males to the younger females, there was four couples. She learned their names, as they were revived. This time she was more prepared for the ordeal of the belt removal, yet it was still excruciating to watch.

Loki lay the one they called Susa in a corner, ordering Tza to guard her, and went to work with Liam, on the males. Shiveron was the first, and possibly the eldest, and as soon as he could stand, he went to his mate, Moriah. Nyle belonged to Twila, who seemed to have suffered the most grievous at the hands of Bom. She had been shaved bald; ears singed black by fire; nose rubbed raw; kicked and bruised, and bones broken.

Tia could almost taste the undercurrent of rage in the beings, as they realized what had been done. It was especially potent when they felt and heard the pain of the women and girls. Tia judged the youngest, Kaudy, to be no more than thirteen or fourteen. Jabek, her partner, was beside himself the moment he realized she'd been manhandled.

It was the same when Reon took note of sixteen year old Iora. The beautiful black girl had in a most ungentle manner, been shorn of her abundant spiral curls, and they lay all about her. Reon screamed with rage at seeing her covered in blood.

But because of weakness, tempers simply cooled, simmering just beneath the surface, as they went to work freeing the others, as quickly as possible.

The ordeal took hours. When at last all could stand, though unsteadily, Shiveron asked the question on everyone's mind:

"How are we going to get home? None of us can teleport, and only you, Liam, have minimal powers."

Now that the others were all free, and Loki could see the positive, he decided to be the encourager. "Water would be good, for starters..."

"We are on the dark side of a dead moon," Liam declared sarcastically. "I doubt you'll find a pool nearby."

"There is a water tap in the kitchen," Tza said without thinking.

Nyle laughed. "Well, who's for a drink?"

"That's not as funny as it sounds," Loki chided. "When I was in the prison, the kitchen was where we found a way out."

Liam grunted disparagingly. "It was Susa who found that, remember? And she's much incapacitated. It's all up to us! With our limited strength and abilities. She dug her way through; I doubt most of us have the energy to even walk far."

That sobered everyone.

"Well," decided Twila. "Let's get that drink at least. I'm dying of thirst."

****

While the others were drinking their fill, some of the younger males went in search of a way out. Reon was first to present any prospect.

"I found a natural vent pipe to the surface, Poppa. We might just be able to climb out?"

Arriving back from searching the tunnels, Liam agreed. "Seeing as Bom has also sealed off the landing bay, that's probably our only hope. Okay, short stuff, let's have a look."

Everyone trailed the two males to a corner of the small kitchen, where just above the cook stove, higher than most could jump, was a perfectly rounded four foot opening in the ceiling.

"It's sheer as far as you can see," Shiveron observed, peering up into the darkness. "And with no hand holds...Are you sure it even leads up?"

"Can't you smell the cold air?" Liam demanded. "Has your broken nose destroyed your olfactory sense?"

"Sorry...guess it has."

"Most of us can jump that high," Nyle put in. "We all have Feline blood mix, but with that circumference, can Loki get through? And what if it narrows up top?"

"I'll do what it takes," Loki said sullenly. "My worry is, the females...especially those badly hurt."

"We can each take our pair female," Liam suggested. "Face to face. One pushes on the up; the other just after; like a clamp and squeeze..."

"Ha! What a wonderful idea," agreed Reon. "Except, there is no way Susa can do that."

"I'll wrap her against me, with my tail," Loki decided. "Her weight is nothing. It'll be like I'm climbing on my own."

"Okay, then," agreed Liam. "I'll take point, in case there is an adversary above. So we only have one more problem..."

He turned to look toward Tza and Tia.

"We have two singles, and you know the rules. So, Tza, what will it be? Will you be responsible for the human?"

"Are we compatible?"

"Most definitely," agreed Loki.

"Then, I will pledge to her gladly," Tza quickly agreed.

"What are you talking about?" Tia demanded, suddenly suspicious.

Liam was the one to explain. "In our society, every female that enters it, must have a protector. A male pledges for life, and may have no other partner...if she accepts his pledge."

"Oh crap! You're selling me like chattel?"

"No. You have a choice..."

"And what if I say no?"

"You may cast him aside...later. But...he will never be permitted to seek another..."

"Oh, for golly sake. Stop beating about the bush," Tza exploded. "Tell the whole truth, Noor! I will be sentenced to death if I prove unsatisfactory."

Tia was horrified.

"Oh, no. No!" she cried out vehemently. "You owe him your lives..."

"And...our capture," reminded Loki.

She caught the small smile as it fleeted across Liam's lips.

Are they teasing or for real?

"Don't look at me," Liam excused, shrugging. "Tza wanted the whole truth out in the open."

Tia turned to Tza. "But I am a human. You are cat!"

The whole crowd hissed at her choice of words.

"We are Feline!" shouted Tza. "Not primitives! We are civilized. You insult us all! You say we are but animals, with nothing but base instincts...humans are better. You are not animalistic?"

"But..."

"Would you rather stay here, female?"

Thoughts of what it would be like alone in this place, left to starve with no food. And the prospect of Bom returning, made her shiver with dread.

"No," she returned pitiably.

"If it is any consolation, I will never touch you that way...unless, it is your desire."

"But...is that even possible?"

Liam chuckled, and broke into the argument. "In our worlds, many males are mated to a human. We have a shortage of females. And every female is most treasured."

"What do I have to do...so he lives?"

"Only accept."

Chapter 15

The two Feline, Thor and Uel, seated in front of the viewer board, stared out the portal at a midnight vastness pinpricked by tiny distant lights. The human, Steven, standing behind them, remarked:

"First time I've actually seen my home planet from this side of the Universe."

The third planet of the system hovered on the horizon, as if it were the satellite instead of the peopled orb, with a population of billions; all blue and green and brown against space; lights twinkling on the surface, blinking back at them.

"Well," stated Thor. "They aren't on that third rock, nor on any others of this system. This moon is the last place to search; our last hope. And they won't be on the light side...too hot for Bom there. So I guess we check the dark side."

"Could they survive in such cold temperatures, without light?" wondered Steven.

"The Noor have an incredible tolerance for all kinds of conditions," Uel disclosed. "But if Bom has them in belts, and has taken out his anger on them..."

"They are alive!" Thor cut in vehemently. "We need to believe that. Let's check behind this cheese ball."

Steven laughed at his choice of words. Since he'd been telling stories of old Earth beliefs, Thor had a habit of coming out with the oddest expressions, as if the legends were fact.

They were just dropping down behind the dark moon, when they spotted a garbage barge coming up over the rise to their left. They decided to follow to see where it was going.

****

The huge disposal transport hovered for a brief moment over the surface of the moon, suspended there like a giant predatory manta ray awaiting its prey. Then it opened huge yawning doors in its belly, and spewed forth the dead on the surface.

"Gross!" Steven exclaimed in disgust. "You mean to say, the Roog have been using our moon as a dump site for their dead?"

Only just now, he noticed the piles of refuge and bones, receding into the distance for miles; no doubt the carnage of ages gone by; each hill range representing eons of past drops.

After vomiting its waste, the disposal craft took off at the speed of light, quickly vanishing from sight.

"Let's see if they have a dock somewhere nearby," Thor suggested, turning their shuttle away, and moving along the surface.

Now that the other ship was gone, he brought up the exterior lights so they could see better. After a time, Uel shouted excitedly.

"There!" He pointed at an indentation in the side of the rocky hill. "What's that?"

"Was a landing bay," agreed Thor. "But it's been imploded from the inside. Those doors will never function again."

"Wasn't done so long ago either," Steven decided. "Does that mean recent activity here?"

"We have long suspected the Roog were using this moon to build warships," Thor admitted. "It's a surprise we haven't come upon these doors sooner, considering how often we've hidden back here ourselves. But, yes, I'd say this attempt at destruction was within the last few weeks."

"Could we get in if we ram them?"

"They are well sealed. Be entirely pointless," stated Thor. "We'd disable our own shuttle and be stuck here."

"And this is probably where Bom took them, right?" Uel surmised.

"More than likely, but..." Thor reasoned. "Bom is long gone. If he left them alive, he left them no way out, you can be sure of that."

"No way he knows of," Uel countered. "Felines can get out when others can't, and they are also Noor. Susa found a way out of the Earth prison..."

"True," agreed Thor. "

"So, how can we help them?"

Peering discouragingly at his monitor, Uel stated the obvious. "No Noor gleam on the screen."

"They'd be in belts, or so severely drained of energy they wouldn't show," Thor decided.

"What we going to do?" persisted Steven.

"We wait," Thor said. "We keep trawling the surface until we spot them coming out."

****

On the ice cold surface, the last deposit of bodies steamed. They were a compilation of life forms: Roog; Feline; half humanoids; Bear and Slither. None stirred. Some seemed very dead; if they weren't, they soon would be.

Many minutes had passed, when from the very center of the pile, a small blue-green snake-like head appeared. The tiny forked red tongue explored the vacuum above, adjusted to the lack of atmosphere, and slithering over its dead companions, the baby lizard body followed the adventurous head.

It soon sensed the warmth coming up from the vent pipe in the ground, made for the hole, curled up next to the edge, to lay waiting, camouflaged a dark color like its surroundings.

****

Liam was the first to crawl from the hole. Even though severely injured himself, he would serve as guardian.

Being in the belt had almost completely disabled his telepathic senses. It was like being physically blind were he human. But he expected no danger out here in zero atmosphere. After all this was a dead abandoned moon.

He was in such bloodied raw physical discomfort, his mental abilities not just deficient but near nonexistent, Liam failed totally to sense that a deadly creature lurked at his back. If the Slither had not been but merely resting, only using its natural instinct to hide, he would have been struck paralyzed the moment he emerged.

Confident that all was safe, he beckoned to Tza to follow, and the Feline, with the human on his back, crept out into the frigid air, scurrying to an overhanging cliff, to shelter beneath. When the two began gasping for breath, it became immediately apparent they were in distress. Liam managed a burst of mental energy, to form a protective bubble of oxygen as protection about the couple.

Then he turned to help Loki from the hole.

The Physical male would have none of relinquishing his burden, and without challenge, Liam allowed him to step away from the edge carrying Susa.

Suddenly sensing danger, Loki quickly lowered his burden to the soil, and turned hissing toward a dark movement at Liam's back. Loki went down in a crouch, snarling protectively, covering the broken form of his female with his own body, preparing to fight this hidden menace.

At last aware they were not alone, Liam moved between his Physical, their mate, and the danger, preparing to take the first blow. When the displaced air began to shimmer, then take shape, he was shocked to see a very young, very angry Slither female in the red color of fight mode.

From her mind, he read the circumstances that had brought her here: the five year old had been orphaned, and taken aboard a troupe transport for sport. In that spilt second, Liam experienced with her the ridicule, abuse and torture at the hands of Roog warriors, until wounded and bleeding, she had crawled away to hide among the dead.

His pity welled up for the unfortunate being, but with the ominous crimson sheen of her scales, Liam had no choice but to fight. The last thing he wanted to do was extend his claws, but instantly, that was what he did. Hissing warningly, the Mental moved to draw the Slither away from the hole and his mates behind him.

At the mouth of the vent hole, the injured, younger, Noor children, and their partners, came out one pair at a time. As each couple escaped the prison, and realized the circumstances existing in their paths, they too went into protection status: all females were herded toward Tza and Tia, with Jabek and his mother, Twila, on guard as the final defense, while the males joined the circle surrounding the enemy. None knew whether there was more than one attacker or not.

It was pitiful to observe. The tiny irate Slither, surrounded by giant Feline Noor, held no chance of survival unless she dropped from attack to compliance. They would be forced to kill her, but none wanted to take her life. And so they milled threateningly about her, hoping her skin color would change.

Only Loki remained at a distance, hovering over the battered form of his mate. He would protect her to the death.

Through the milling circle, the Slither suddenly caught sight of the broken form on the ground.

Here was the most vulnerable of the pack.

But she did not appear to consider attack. Instead, she went rigid, and for long moments stood frozen. She watched the still form at Loki's knees, while everyone else held their breath.

From her mind, Liam saw her relate to the helpless, injured state of this victim. Something in the sight of the still hopeless form broke through the fear and anger in the tiny creature.

She is bonding to Susa!

Her scales changed from vibrant red to dark forest green and finally to a comfortable shade of blue-green.

Liam immediately gave the mental command:

Stand down!

All males in the circle dropped to a crouch; even Loki calmed his stance, trustingly stepping back from Susa's still form.

The Slither female eased to the ground, slowly inched forward on her belly. All knew she wasn't hunting, for on the ship of Dia, where most had been raised, the human cross Slithers were friends, protectors. The Noor were familiar with their ways.

When a Slither attaches to any being, it is for life. The only time the Noor family had seen that happen before was when their Slither pair, Sith and Serene, had attached to the younger Noor as babies. To attach meant they would protect them for life.

That was what was happening now. Aware, this Noor female was the most vulnerable, the young Slither female was inching forward to bond with the unconscious Susa. By its opinion, she was in the most need of her protection.

The males from the circle moved with her, just in case their assessment was wrong, stepping aside to let her pass, yet staying close enough to stop the Slither should she turn the color of red fight mode again.

As she came abreast of Loki, he hissed a warning, stating his right to be with Susa, but the infant Slither simply ignored him. When he hissed a second time, she bravely hissed back, but only as a warning, as if to state her claim, or to say, 'I don't wish to fight you.'

When she reached Susa, the Slither moved along the broken right leg, crawled across, to attach; like a small silver ankle bracelet, it curled around her left calf, and went invisible. From that point on, she would only show herself as living, if someone she was unfamiliar with approached. To all intents and purposes, if you saw her at all, she appeared to be an ornament Susa wore.

But Loki quickly realized, as Susa's mate, even he would have to earn the trust of the small deadly Slither. As he tried to lay down beside his mate, she rose up and hissed at him warningly.

From the young reptile's mind, Liam found out her name: Oona. Loki, as a Physical himself, found her weakness. A hungry Slither in protection mode would not hunt for herself.

He easily caught a non-air breathing rat from the refuse pile. When he held it out, Oona fed, after which, she allowed Loki to rest spoon-like behind his mate.

Together the group settled down to await rescue. None were in any condition to heal themselves or another. For the others, there was no food or drink. Liam only had enough mental strength to maintain a safe bubble shield for all; there was no air or light.

They slept to ease their pain, and prolong what little life they had left in them.

Surely, someone must be looking for them.

Chapter 16

The first Tia was aware they had been rescued was when she opened her eyes to a large hospital-like expanse; the walls were bright, of some sort of metallic material, and she was lying in a white sheeted bed that was too big for her. Like an IV on Earth, on her right wrist, was a small glowing cylinder of glass and metal that seemed to be feeding her, though she could not see any line leading away out of it.

For some time she simply lay there and listened to the sounds around her: beeping machines; groans in the distance, other voices, the words and the language too far away to interrupt.

A being resembling Tza floated by, but it was not walking, it glided just above the surface floor, obviously not flesh and blood but a machine, a robot attendant. Finally it came to her side, checked the cylinder on her wrist, then carried on to another patient beyond her vision. Tia surmised, she was in some sort of hospital.

When I am strong again, what do they plan to do with me? Will they eat me, as the dog creatures would?

Sudden terror flooded her system; goose bumps prickled her skin; her breathing turned rapid.

What do I really know about these giants? Who says I can trust them? They might be lying, for all I know. Now that they are free and safe, why should they keep their promises?

Visions of white robed shadow figures dissecting her warm body while she was still conscious danced in her head.

Just an experiment to see what makes me tick...

She almost screamed in her panic.

No, I'm not going to wait around for them to do that! It's time to get out of here!

She sat up, slipped her feet over the side. A small ladder appeared along the side of the cot, dropping down to the floor.

Apparently, she wasn't confined.

When her feet touched the floor, her legs gave way in weakness. For a moment, she just sat there; then rather than risk walking, she crawled away beneath the cots until she found a doorway. No one noticed as she eased back against the wall, inside, by a corner, to rest.

****

It seemed, she was now in what appeared to be a large operating room. On a stool, near a raised table, sat Loki. He still seemed inattentive, lethargic, as if he was hardly able to function due to weariness, but still he was intently focused on the battered figure on the table, the female Noor they called Susa.

Behind the table, also on a stool, was Liam. He appeared totally out of it, panting in pain, his wounds unattended, still festering and bleeding. His eyes were closed as though, somehow, he was trying to give energy to the small figure at the center of their attention, whose hand he held.

A third being was present, a man-sized cat creature. He stood, back to Tia, bending over the patient on the table. He must have worn a translator, because she could understand his words easily, and obviously, he was a physician.

"I've never physically had to repair a Noor before. You've always healed yourselves," he stated. "You are certain, even Loki has no healing power?"

"With Tilk down, the whole Noor family has no powers, Kimon," Liam revealed wearily. "I can't even transfer energy to Susa."

"Then how am I to treat her?"

"She's part human. Treat her body like that of a human..."

"Operate the primitive way!" Kimon gasped with disbelief.

"Yes. You will have to..."

Kimon shivered visible. "How barbaric!"

Then, he stooped over the patient to examine more closely.

"The fractures, I can set...she's blind...I don't think I can repair the eyes; they are loose in the sockets..."

"A stitch in the muscle area..." suggested Liam.

Kimon murmured agreement. "The eyes are her power, aren't they? She'll never be the powerful being she once was..."

"No! Correction. Tilk operates through her eyes...until Tilk can come out, we will remain powerless...but...Susa will heal..." Liam broke down, unable to speak for a moment. "Do what you can for the Physical; we will use water for the rest."

Kimon nodded, then shook his head again. "I have no idea what to do with this wing. I've never seen such a Noor advancement in a living being before. The wings are a sign of royal Noor blood."

"I would suggest bracing it against her back, so the bones knit together. Strap it until the muscles grow stronger..."

"She will have excruciating pain...when she tries to stretch it out..."

"Loki already is one with her pain..."

"I am not certain he can endure much more of that..."

There was silence in the room, as Kimon continued to go over his patient.

"You realize her back is broken in three places," the physician finally said. "Just above the hips, between the shoulder blades, and up at the neck...a brace until the bones knit? Will she ever walk again?"

"She'll walk...she'll run; she'll beat me again!" Loki broke in from his corner. And then he began to weep softly.

****

Tia must have fallen asleep then. When next she opened her eyes, she was back in a bed with Tza lying behind her.

Chapter 17

"Can you swim, Tia?"

The Japanese nodded at Liam's query.

"Then come into the bath with us. You too Tza. We need you to stand guard."

Tia expected stalls or at least a tub; what she saw, as she stepped into the huge room, was something quite different. At the center was a rectangular pool of at least sixty feet long, forty wide and ten feet deep. From the far end a waterfall poured, entering about half way up the wall. The way the water in the pool churned constantly, she gathered, it was recycled, and the falls was its entry point. The liquid steamed, obvious evidence it was warm; she never expected hot.

"Strip," ordered Liam.

By now, Tia was used to obeying; it took but a minute, and she stood waiting in the buff.

"I'll take first turn, Loki," Liam offered.

Loki nodded, sat down on the edge. "Oona, come!"

Susa lay unconscious at Liam's feet. Suddenly on her ankle appeared the tiny bracelet shape of the Slither predator. Oona unclasped, and quickly slithered to Loki, where she vanished abruptly.

Tia standing naked, gave a shiver.

Every day I've helped with Susa; I never realized that deadly thing was ever present...like some malevolent spirit watching over her.

Liam caught his mate up in his arms; slid into the water. "Tia, while we're under, acclimatize yourself with the water. At some point, I may need you to hold her for me."

Then he dove, taking Susa still unconscious, under, along with him.

Tia forgot his order, gasping in fear.

"He'll drowned her!"

"A Noor can breathe under water," Loki said quietly. "Better enter the pool slowly...it'll be hot to you."

Stunned by his revelation, Tia failed to hear. Without thinking, she dived head first into the pool after Liam. And came up screaming, then held her breath until the burning subsided.

Standing guard over by the door, Tza scolded. "Why didn't you stop her, Physical? You could have at least cooled the water."

Loki sighed despondently. "I tried. Have enough pain to deal with..." he grumbled.

Liam surfaced, and realizing what had happened, added his word to the admonishment.

"Loki, take Susa!" His tone left no argument, and Loki dove in, switching places quickly; disappearing with the injured patient beneath the waves.

"Do you need a healing salve?" Liam asked of Tia.

"I'm okay...now. It was my own fault. I didn't listen..."

"Preventable...don't know why Loki didn't..." Liam sighed. "Of course...he's overwhelmed with Susa. I shouldn't have jumped on him, too."

****

Loki stayed under with Susa a long, long time. Finally, his head broke the surface with a crash, as if he couldn't hold his breath a moment longer, but being Noor, breathing wasn't the problem.

"Your turn, Liam," he ordered curtly. "I need...a break."

"Go," agreed the Mental, joining him in the pool, catching up the limp female form, and diving.

Tia tread water, waiting to be of use, as Loki climbed slowly over the edge, to sit there. At first she simply watched the shadowy, shimmering forms below, waiting for them to surface once more, but perhaps a muted noise drew her attention. She turned, and looked at Loki.

He was bent double, his hands over his face, shoulders shaking. Shocked, Tia realized, the giant Noor Physical was silently sobbing.

Seldom in her life had Tia seen a man cry. The men of her family were private individuals; they would never let the women see them lose control. Yet, in Tia's eyes, the very fact, she was witnessing the mighty male's breaking point, made him seem that much more approachable. She somehow knew, his tears were not from the scolding of his companions; they were from an overload of all that was happening...or not happening, with the woman beneath the water. Compassion for him, tore at Tia's heart.

So intent was she on the grieving Loki, she failed to realize Liam had broken above the water with Susa, until the Mental male spoke.

"Tia," Liam ordered softly. "Come hold Susa's head above the water, for a moment."

She quickly swam over, wrapped her arms under the unconscious woman's arms. Liam moved to the ledge, pulled himself up beside his Physical, and gathered Loki against him.

"Junction, Loki!" he ordered abruptly.

Loki moaned, gasped in a sob, and swallowed deeply. "Not here. We need to be alone."

"Doesn't matter. Do it! You need it now."

What happened next, nearly made Tia let go her water. Suddenly, there was only one male, where there had been two: a nine foot tall giant, a combination of both Liam and Loki.

Tia gave an involuntary yelp, and nearly let Susa slip beneath the water.

He was enormous, colossal, muscular and solid; his features, hands, and feet were still humanoid. The hair was a combination of dark-silver and red-gold curls; the Feline eyes were turquoise with a bronzed vertical slit center. Now a ten foot sleek shorthaired tail was like a shadow, barely visible, as it curved along from behind him, and into the water. This new being had to weigh at least a thousand pounds.

Who is that? And where did he come from?

She heard Tza gasp in startled horror; leave his post, and rush forward. As he stepped closer, Tza dropped to his knees. There seemed no fear in him, only awe.

"Master...you are...one...male?"

Liam/Loki laughed self consciously. "Yes, Tza. This is our natural look, our junctioned form. Not many have witnessed it. They fear too much. You'll keep our secret...okay? Now...if you'll just give us a moment to balance... Return to your post...please."

"Sorry...sorry," Tza excused, backing once again toward the sliding entry doors, where he stood rigidly at attention, as if he somehow had been reprimanded.

Long moments of heavy silence followed. and then the one became two once again.

"Okay, now?" Liam asked of Loki.

The Physical nodded.

"Am I safe to leave you and go get Susa?"

"Yes," Loki agreed. "I'm sorry I lost it."

"You feel the pain more than I do...it makes the heartache much harder...your breakdown is understandable."

"I'm good. Go! We need to analyze...if it has done any good."

****

"Ready, Instant Healer?" queried Liam.

Nodding, Loki placed his hand on their battered mate.

"The one heart is now beating strong; the second is like a shadow behind, gives an extra beat at every five to eight of the other. I think the second heart will repair also...it will take time. The body we can work with..."

"But?"

"Oh, Liam...the brain. It is so damaged. They will be scarred."

****

Day after day, the water treatment was repeated. And after each session, it seemed there was no visible change. Susa remained in what humans might call a coma, her outward body braced with transparent braces; over the wounded wing, along the broken limbs, and down the back, from head to the beginning of the tail. Across her eyes, the bandage also was see-through.

Many times, both the Noor males seemed despondent, but never again was there need for them to junction. Now that Tia and Tza were considered trustable, they were always the chosen helpers at the pool. They had been privy to the deepest secrets of the Junction pair male, and had not betrayed them.

Chapter 18

Tia had been moved into an ante with Tza, where it was hoped, being alone with him, they would get to know each other.

When she was with him, she always felt safe. As they cuddle-slept naked together, his silken fur against her body no longer felt alien.

It now seemed, as if Earth had never existed, and human kind had not been her ancestry. She no longer feared the dead of her family. She felt certain, that those that had passed ahead of her, seeing her safety and happiness, were at peace, and that was all that mattered.

Tza had left the sleep mat earlier, leaving her curled in a soft wrap, while he went to check on what was planned for the day. Now he came hurriedly in, seeming disconcerted.

"They want us to serve as attendants on the floor today. They are short staffed, they say, because the Noor Healers are incapacitated. Hurry and dress."

Tza was protective of her when others challenged, yet his manner toward her in private was still hesitant and shy. When he saw her naked, he averted his eyes, but she knew, every chance he got, when she turned her back, he snuck a peek.

****

On the highest observation deck of the vast medical bay, Spafford prowled. The junior Physician was annoyed, angry; beyond provoked. When the Healers had returned, he had expected things to return to normal, but instead, they had taken privilege, as if they were patients.

In his opinion, the whole war situation was the fault of these cross-breeds. Some said, what was wrong with them was a hereditary anomaly, but the minor Physician had done research. They had a blood disease, a plague that affected only certain types. Spafford felt, it needed to be eradicated.

Yet these choice few were treated as special, given privilege, held above, as if they were of importance, all because Dia and Kimon protected them; because the eldest were cousin/ grandsons to Kei.

But Kei is dead now! The battle we fight is because of that she, the males brought back with them!

And, rumor was the she was too battered to fix, anyway.

Why even try? They should put her out of her misery!

For the convenience of the Physicians watching what went on below, a railed deck ran all around the bay. Beneath this stretched many levels of transparent staggered floors, each with innumerable beds, every one containing a patient, usually male, a wounded warrior from battle, who had fought, been injured; deserved attention.

What is the point to their bravery? Felines will not normally fight unless cornered; they would rather run or hide. Dog will always hate cat, but for these privileged Noor, the infected of Dia, we are fighting a meaningless battle.

Yet, Spafford knew he dare not voice his thoughts. Kimon was the male in charge.

There had been a day when the head Physician was in agreement, but for some reason, Kimon had been swayed to the other side. Spafford despised and loathed him for his cowardice, his inconsistency.

Spafford watched, as below the Mechanicals cleaned around the beds, administered the meds to the ailing, and injured. On the board beside him, a duty requiring an actual

Physician, was displayed. He shivered. It was for the Noor female.

I don't need Loki present, if I take this...

He quickly sent an order for the Physical to meet Liam at the baths.

That should get rid of him for a time. All that lazy Healer wants to do, since he came back, is sleep beside his female! Well, I'll have none of that!

Spafford indicated, he would take the duty himself.

****

"Female!" growled Spafford, as he passed Tia. "Get over here! I need your assistance."

Leaping deftly to Susa's cot, he straddled the patient, a knee on either side.

"Well, did you hear me?" he bellowed impatiently.

Tia scurried to the head of the bed.

"What are you going to do to her?"

"Not that it is your business to question a Physician," he hissed. "But this patient needs her nose repacked, so it will heal straight. Otherwise the organ will be useless..."

"You are not suppose to do anything without one of the Noor males present. Where did Loki go?"

"I sent that lazy male to the baths; he'll only get in the way. I don't need his interference! Since he came back, he is useless as a Healer. All he wants to do is lie beside his female and sleep. No good as a Healer anymore! Hold her head, will you!"

When Tia was too slow to react, he growled ominously: "Are you stupid, too, human? I can have you deported in an instant; sent to the Slave planet, where humans belong..."

Tia had been sleep trained on the computer board, but also as a minor medic. The things this male said about Loki irked her, for she did know something about the function of an Instant Healer; Loki was absorbing Susa's pain, and that was why he tended to sleep so much. Yet she was timid; not wishing to confront openly.

She was always curious to learn more, wishing to prove herself; usually, she silently watched without interfering. However, this Physician seemed unusually callous and rough. She felt his method was unnecessary.

Spafford had Susa face up. He had removed the packing from her nose, and now was ramming with a firm rod and brutal force, the clean strips, up the nose. With each forceful shove, the unconscious body jerked from the strength of the effort, and the victim moaned, as if feeling each blow.

This is not right!

"Tza!" screamed Tia. "Tza!"

Where is that male when I need him?

"You shut up, human!" Spafford hissed irately. "Or you will be out of here so fast..."

"What is going on here?" demanded Tza, arriving suddenly at their side.

"Don't think you can interfere, guardian," growled Spafford. "You have no say here."

"What's happening , Tia?" Tza wanted to know.

"He sent Loki away, so he wouldn't be able to interfere..."

"You better not interfere either, male. I'll see you are put out of this bay so fast..."

"I know this much," Tza objected. "Nothing is suppose to be done on this female without her males present..."

"Shows how much you really know..." returned Spafford, jarring another ream of padding home. "Get out of here, before I show you who's boss!"

Tza spun on his heel, and fled, leaving Tia alone to deal with the situation.

"Now that we have that dealt with..." Spafford ordered. "Hold...her...head!"

Hesitantly, Tia complied.

When Susa began to thrash, Spafford knelt on her hands.

"You don't be still, Noor," he hissed in her ear. "I'll kneel on your broken arm; see how you like that!"

"Can't you see?" Tia defended. "She can't breathe...at least give her freezing for the pain..."

"Oh, I suppose, you are an authority, now?" Spafford chided. "I'll have you know, drugs are useless on the Noor. When they work at all, they have an opposite effect. Hold her!"

"She's choking!"

"So what! Nature will take over. She'll either expire or revive in time..."

And suddenly, the defiant physician was suspended in mid air at the end of Liam's gigantic arm.

"You have tortured my female for the last time!" thundered the Noor Mental.

Then gently, he set the Physician back to the floor.

"Where is Loki?" Liam asked calmly. "And the Slither guardian, Oona?"

Spafford was trembling visibly. "I misdirected him; sent him to the baths; ordered him to take any guard with him."

"Crafty," hissed Liam. "Come with me."

"The board...said her packing needed replacing," objected Spafford.

"And was the attitude part of the order? It seems to me, if what I read from your mind, your opinion of the human, and Healer clans makes you unfit to serve on this ship at all..."

While the two males argued, and moved into the distance, Tia began stroking the hair of the unconscious Noor female. Soon, Tia felt her relax, as if somehow, Susa knew she was not alone; that finally, she had a protector.

The patient sighed, and slipped deeper into coma.

When Tia looked up again, Liam was just returning, after escorting the errant Physician off the floor.

"Tia; Tza," Liam ordered, gently shifting Susa to his arms. "Join me in the baths..."

As they followed him, Tia dared to ask a question.

"He said, he could have me sent to the Slave planet, where I belong...can he do that?"

"He will not be doing anything," Liam returned quietly. "He has been banned from the ship; will be leaving for Jump Central directly. He will be no more trouble to you...

"And," he added. "You both are in our service. No one has any say in your discipline, save us."

Chapter 19

They floated in a sea of agony and confusion, hiding in memories of places and things more pleasant. The Essence held the other; the other's spirit near non-existent.

It's okay Susa. You are not alone. We have each other.

I am afraid. It hurts too much. I want to give up, just go away...

I have you...don't let go.

The body is too painful. I need to leave it. I am afraid to go back, Tilk...it will...hurt.

Just rest a little longer with me.

Invisible arms gently tightened; love-feeling passed from one to the other.

This time, I do not intend to abandoned this body I chose, and seek another. You have been too brave. I will not cast you aside. If you cannot fight any longer, I will die with you. It is time. The battle has been long...time to finish it.

The Essence Being resolved this, kissing the forehead of the suffering soul in her arms.

No, Tilk...let me go...alone.

Never! You have gone through too much for me; I will not abandon you. It is time to finish this, once and for all!

I...cannot be the end of you...let me sleep just a little while longer. I do not yet have the courage to go back to the real world. Hold me...I am so...cold.

****

Weeks later Tia was gently brushing Susa's hair after a session in the water. Loki was curled behind the Noor female, in a sleep of deep exhaustion, while Liam was some distance away, talking quietly with Kimon.

Distantly, Tia could hear the two males discussing the wisdom of continuing. They had removed the eye wrappings to give the patient a break, but the lids were still closed; not even a flutter.

Oh, don't give up on her; not just yet. It will kill Loki...

Tia had become rather fond of the male pair. She grieved for them. And had become almost a silent advocate to the suffering coma patient. It would be hard to let her go.

As Tia brushed, it seemed, Susa had moved her head out of the comfortable positioning where Tia had placed it. Gently, the Japanese girl turned the chin, and continued brushing again.

Finally finished, Tia lowered the head, and moved off the couch, to put the brush away. When she turned back, she gave a sharp involuntary squeal. Susa's eyes were open, and staring straight at her.

The pupil of the eye was non-existent; the iris a continual shifting of constantly changing multi-rainbow hues, unlike anything she had ever seen before.

Liam was abruptly beside her, with Kimon not far behind. And Loki rose up startled, a bit confused, but suddenly wide awake.

The Physical straddled his female, his knees on either side of her. Susa's eyes turned slowly toward him.

Loki turned her on her back.

"Do you know me, little one?" he asked hopefully.

"My children?" hissed, barely audible, through the locked, braced jaw.

Loki bent, and gently kissed the perspiring forehead, barely holding in check the delight he was feeling.

"So good to have you back," he whispered softly.

Again, the urgent question. "My children?"

"All safe, though slow to recuperate."

The eyes closed; the body relaxed, and the battered Noor female slipped away again, but this time only to slumber.

****

The days that came after her awakening were by no means easy. Susa was still physically blind. The phenomena Tia and the others had seen had simply been the manifestation of the Essence Tilk.

It was hard to look at Susa sometimes. One eye looked forward, the other tracked to the side; the nose was still pushed in and up, flat somewhat, and her breathing was labored.

How could this Being have been as powerful as it is rumored?

Her body was so broken; the twisted limbs, if not for the back brace, would not have supported her. Even with more water treatments, progress was slow.

Her speech came halting, and thought processes hesitant. Sometimes, she would be standing there, and suddenly blank out, as if the mechanisms inside her brain had stopped. Then Loki would reach out, touch the top of her head, before she collapsed in the stupor, and instead, he would be the one to fold slowly against the bench, taking on the brain malfunction to heal it.

At times, it would take but minutes for him to recover, other times hours. Then both he, and Susa would sleep again, spoon-like, he behind her.

Chapter 20

One day Tilk/Susa summoned the fleet commander. The Feline was a proud male, comfortable and confident in his position. He expected respect, and was somewhat unimpressed, when upon his arrival, he found the lady dozing.

He stood there waiting impatiently. Guarded by her Physical mate, she seemed to be unapproachable, until Loki gently roused her.

"You sent for the fleet commander; he is here for his audience."

"Ah, yes." The first words were spoken aloud, with difficulty, through a jaw that had obviously been broken, and braced shut to heal. After that, she communicated telepathically, the words sounding in his mind.

She surprised him, by asking not about the state of the war effort, but about an inconsequential planet, where the prison system had existed.

"What are the conditions of the Forbidden Planet?"

He hesitated only a second; though astonished, he was not caught off guard. He had come prepared for most anything.

"The planet itself is in self-destruct: earthquakes, continual super volcanic eruptions, severe weather patterns of all kinds. Their food chain is destroyed; atmosphere and most water sources polluted. The breathable air quality is at ten percent. Most human government leaders have gone into underground bunkers, leaving the general populace to fend for itself. A small group of the more affluent of these, has gone into bio-spheres, but these structures are doomed to fail, as the surface beneath is breaking apart. The creatures, both human and animal, have a death sentence upon them."

He had given all this in a monotone recital, as if the fate of those of whom he spoke, did not concern him.

Susa nodded her head slightly, and switched topics.

"And what of the Roog?"

"They have vacated the surface. They hang in ships above the doomed world, transferring down to hunt for hours at a time, then returning to their carriers to sleep..."

"And where is our fleet?"

Finally, she was interested in the battle, which as he saw it, was of most importance.

"We stay near the entrance to the solar system, to prevent them escape, and to thwart any others from joining them. We have not considered it wise to engage those inside; our ships would become trapped..."

"Brave males, aren't you?" she stated succinctly, and he had the distinct feeling, she was coldly angry. "Easy to stay out of harm's way. We have taken many casualties?"

"Yes, my Lady. Look around you; this med ship, as are many others, is full to capacity with the injured."

She hissed at him, and he stepped back in shock.

"Do not be insolent, male. I believe you know, Kei appointed me to succeed her. You will pay the respect due me, or I will have you replaced. Understood?"

He nodded, and bowed from the waist.

"My present condition does not mean I am powerless..."

"My apologies, my Lady..."

"Now, that we understand each other, here are my commands; tell those under you, this is a message direct from their Queen. I was raised on the Planet we have been discussing, and that race of humans is dear to my heart. As for the many Feline's injured and lost, this also greatly grieves me. From this point on, the Feline fleet will defend themselves only; they will not instigate or initiate an encounter with the enemy. Our main effort will be focused on the rescue of the human population of the Forbidden Planet..."

His jaw nearly dropped at this statement, and as he realized what this entailed, he lost all his proud composer. "But, my Lady...that will mean, we must enter the solar system. We will become trapped!"

"You will not be trapped! If you moved your entire fleet to surround the third planet, and jump the beings out to Jump Center, where our second armada waits..."

Again, he was flabbergasted. She had knowledge even he did not have.

"Tell me, warrior," Susa demanded. "What is the value of our lives, if we watch a budding, though primitive race of humanoids, the largest group of such intelligent creatures in existence, be eradicated, while we do nothing? Are we not as guilty as the Roog, if we do not help them?"

He was silent for a moment, pondering. When he replied, his wisdom was evident.

"We as a race, would be shamed, as guilty of genocide as the dogs. At present, our war with them is merely a selfish one, a war of sham and self preservation."

"Exactly," Susa agreed.

"My Lady," he asked at last. "What are we to do with these peoples? What is your desire?"

"All are to be treated as equals. No preferential treatment to their leaders; the lesser is the same as those who have been governing...the same, as it is among all species out here in the Universe."

"And...what of the Roog? Are we to take captives?"

"If you find yourselves with Roog prisoners, they are to be treated with dignity, their wounds tended, but...they are not to be fed human meat, and yes, it would be wise to keep them confined, until they can be tried for their crimes. Be especially careful when you encounter Bom. And Clio is also to be considered an Enemy of the deadliest caliber.

As soon as either of the last are encountered, give no quarter or privilege."

"Understood." He bowed then, knowing he was being dismissed. "My Lady!" he added, approval and a new respect in his tone. He stepped back, turned, and moved away.

****

By the time the rescue began, there was nothing left of government on the planet; thieves and murderers ruled the surface. Yet, when the Felines came down, the population feared and fought their efforts, thinking their purpose the same as the Roog.

Felines risk life and limb on two sides: the Roog did everything possible to prevent human rescue, killing both human and Feline. The humans fled whenever possible, and Felines finally gave up the effort to convince any humanoid, they were friendlies. They simply captured them, and beamed them aboard the ships.

On board the ships, the system was better, although they more or less resorted to a prison-like set up. At first, each human found themselves confined, but as they gradually realized they were not being viewed as supper, they relaxed, and followed orders, more or less obediently, depending upon the temperament of the individual.

A human, when it entered the system, was treated as most other beings: analyzed, taught, fitted with a translator, and given temporary lodging and work duty. Until this war with the Roog ended, the human situation could not be fully dealt with either.

The Planet surface below deteriorated to the point, it was about to explode. The ships above pulled away, and any who had fought rescue to the end, perished in the final death throws with the home they held so dear.

Chapter 21

"Lady...open eyes," ordered the mechanical Feline orderly. "Need drops."

Tia, standing nearby, heard Susa hiss at the annoying machine.

"Need drops," insisted the artificial orderly.

It never ceased to amaze Tia how lifelike the mechanicals were. The only way she could tell some of them from the real beings, was by their inability to display genuine compassion.

"Need drops," insisted the orderly. "Open eyes."

"Go away," hissed Susa. "Or I'll send you away."

****

To this point, her healing process had mostly involved sleeping, but as her body began to mend, Susa found herself awake more, depressed, and chaffing to be released from the hospital proper. Even though the wards were open, and spacious, she felt confined, closed in, and claustrophobic.

She was always aware of the constant eyes upon her, and the many minds were hard to shut away. Not a moment was private; there was nowhere she could be alone to find her peace.

She longed to be free, but the braces controlled her movements, and the many strangers invaded her thoughts. She found it almost impossible to balance her emotions, and so her short temper flared more than once.

****

"Need drops."

"Don't need drops!" growled Susa.

"Need drops to repair eyes..."

"Water does that for us; don't treat me like a human!"

"Orders say; need drops."

"Like hell! What do you know, you stupid machine!"

Rounding the corner, with Loki at his side, Kimon was just in time to see the mechanical abruptly vanish from view.

"Susa!" thundered the head Physician. "Did you just destroy that mechanical?"

"No!" growled Susa. "I sent him to his cubical."

"What's the matter with you, that you won't cooperate? You need your eyes lubricated. I'll put the drops in myself, then."

"They burn..." protested Susa.

As Kimon took another bottle from the shelf above them, and approached the bed, Susa's temper flared, and in barely audible tones, she told him what to do with the medication.

"What was that?" Kimon inquired.

"Put them where the sun don't shine..." the Noor female repeated.

Loki chuckled.

"What's so funny?" asked Kimon in annoyance. "I suppose, you could do better with her?"

"I don't need the drops," declared Susa adamantly.

"Yes, you do," disagreed Kimon.

"They are for humans! I am mixed..."

"We are treating this way, and that's that!" declared the head Physician. "Now, cooperate!"

"Go to hell!"

"You need to listen to her," Loki defended. "She knows her own body..."

"Did I ask for your help, male?" Susa interjected, turning on her Physical mate irritably. "I can handle my own battles, thank you very much."

"Testy, aren't we, today?"

Tears sprang to her eyes at the rebuke.

Kimon broke in. "Fine. If you think the drops are unnecessary, tell me what is needed."

"Water!" Susa hissed. "Just water!"

"Very well, Loki take her to the baths."

"I don't need you! I can do it myself."

Susa dropped down off the bed, steadying herself with a hand on the side of the cot. Loki reached out, but she stubbornly batted him away.

"Leave me alone! I can manage on my own."

Loki shrugged, stepped away, motioned with his hand for Tia to go with Susa.

"I saw that," Susa declared indignantly. "I'm not mentally blind, as well."

"How?" questioned Tia of Loki. "How can she see?"

"Oh, didn't you know? I've got eyes in the back of my head, human."

Tia's eyes went wide. Without thinking it through, the words came out in a rush. "Where? I've been brushing your hair all this time, and I've never seen them..."

Loki exploded with laughter.

"Stupid!" hissed Susa. "I can see through your mind, from your eyes. Now, leave me be. All of you!"

But at a nod from Loki, Tia followed her; at a safe distance, anyway.

****

When she got into the baths, Tia found Susa at the water's edge, sobbing brokenly. She ran to her, gathering her into her arms.

"Oh, honey. It's got to get better," she crooned. "It won't always be like this. It's okay. It'll be okay."

"Never...be...okay. Never again," sobbed Susa. "This is worse than when I was totally human. At least, then...I could physically see..."

"But, that will heal...at least, that's what the men say..." Then to distract her, Tia approached the implication voiced prior. "What do you mean, 'when you were human'?"

Susa brushed at her tears, gulped back a sob. "Once, I was just as human as you. I was captured by the Roog, taken into their prison as a breeder..."

For only a second, Tia doubted her, but she had seen much since she herself had been captured. Anything was possible, in this world.

"Bom's prison?" she gasped, shocked.

"Yes. I nearly died there..." Susa seemed to reflect on the reality. "I guess, it wasn't so good being human, either..."

In sudden agreement, Tia laughed. Then marveling, she asked: "But...how come...you look like you do now?"

"Loki was physician; a prisoner, as well. He was told to dispose of me; I was near death. But...instead, he transfused me with his own blood. He was in a drain belt, and unable to Instant Heal because of it."

"His blood...did this to you? Made you like them?"

"I would be dead, if he hadn't. Sometimes...I wish they'd let me die..."

"Would you kill all of us in the process, as well?" Loki's voice challenged from just behind them at the door. Each woman had been so intent on the other, neither had heard the barrier slide open and then shut.

Susa hissed, and raised her head rebelliously. "No males! I need privacy! Leave!"

"You don't need to be alone," Loki differed. "That is the worst thing for you at this moment."

"Stay away!" growled Susa.

Her body began to send out small static blue and red bolts of visible energy.

"Move away from her, Tia," warned Loki. "Do it now!"

Frightened by the urgency in the large male's tone, Tia rose, and ran for the door.

"No, Tia," cautioned Loki. "Stay in the room. You need to obey me...without question."

Complying, just short of the door, Tia dropped to her knees, covering her head defensively, whimpering fearfully.

The sound of an electric charge building, made her look up again, and sit dumbfounded, mouth agape.

Susa was glowing, sending out sparks, the rivulets of light running across her body like a neon sign light show. Oona, her tiny Slither guardian, broke free from the flashing Noor's ankle, and disappeared safely in a far corner of the room.

Loki dropped to his knees, waiting, as if this were not an unusual thing. After Susa seemed to calm, and the phenomena abated, Loki finally spoke:

"Am I so offensive, you would repulse me with such a charge?"

Tears began to travel unchecked down the Noor female's cheeks, but she said nothing.

"May I come near you, female?" Loki pleaded. "Let me give comfort."

A nod, ever so slight, gave him permission.

But Loki didn't stand up, and walk to her. Instead, he stayed on his knees, crawled close, and as if in submission, he lowered his head, moved his arms along the tiles toward her, similar to a bow.

"May I touch?" he asked quietly.

All sign of the static had disappeared, but the tears still flowed silently. She nodded again.

As he gathered her in his arms to cuddle her close, Susa cried plaintively:

"I want to go home, Loki. Take me out of this infirmary; I'm so tired of being a sideshow, a curiosity for the other patients to gossip about."

He stroked her hair gently, trying to soothe her. "I know, little one. I feel it, too," he agreed sympathetically.

"I want these braces removed from my body. How can the bones heal, if never let free?"

He nodded against her soft head.

Liam materialized beside them, dropping to his knees. He remained quietly, like a protective guardian, until Loki spoke to him.

"She's had all she can take of this forced integration; the primitive medical treatment... Kimon will not listen to me...he fixates on one method, and won't let it go..."

"We could just leave," suggested Liam. "Take her to home planet..."

"She would never survive the trip," Loki stated. "Nor would we. Our energy stems out of hers now, since we were so deeply balancing one another..."

"And so our powers are dependent upon her, as well," Liam added. "The strength of all, depends always on her vigor...what is your wish, little Tusha?"

A small smile flit across the strained face; the lips slightly curled with pleasure.

"I haven't heard that for a while. How repulsive, and battered, is this butterfly...dying...with a broken wing..."

"Never unattractive to me," both males declared quickly in unison.

"Home," pleaded Susa. "Away from all the injured, and puzzled minds. To Dia's bed nest. If we go there, maybe Kimon won't be so angry at our going. Maybe, he will let my family leave the hospital then, also."

Loki agreed. "We'll just discharge ourselves!"

"And Tia?" Susa queried. "And Tza...they can move in with us, too?"

The males grinned, and looked to Tia.

"Would you like to join our family nest?"

Uncertain what that entailed, Tia hesitated.

"Tza!" Liam sent out the mental command. "Join us in the female bath house."

Seconds later, the outside doors slid open; Tza stepped in.

"You called, sir?"

Suddenly, all were in a very large, spacious chamber separated into two sections, each with enormous floor mats, obviously meant to serve a group sleeping arrangement.

"Soo...tired," moaned Susa.

And, as if all were of one mind, the three Noor curled up in each other's arms, and were immediately asleep.

Tza grinned, seeming to know what had happened. He led Tia to the other mat, and they followed suit.

Later, sleepily, Tia realized they had been joined by many others: Susa's family, a few humans, two Bear, and many Feline. Yet she felt too weary to care or complain. Actually, the closeness was comforting.

Chapter 22

Bom paced the circular observation walkway, that ran around the entire outer rim of the ship he had commandeered from the fleet, as his own.

He was livid with rage. He now knew, the Noor were again at liberty, had somehow escaped the burial death-trap he had left them in. He simply didn't know where they were now. He suspected, they most likely, had taken refuge on Dia's med ship.

However, he was now banned from any sort of entry at that facility.

Out beyond the view ports, Bom could see the vast Roog fleet, a mighty flotilla of battle ready ships. One by one, they were picking off the Feline ships that guarded the med ships.

It seemed strange to Bom, though these cat ships were surrounded, they would not engage or initiate the fight, only defend. As a result, the Felines were taking many casualties.

In the very middle of this unbalanced array, were the large medical transports, protected by the insignia of the neutral medical association, serving always to care for the injured of any side. Dia's ship was at this center; a bastion of hope for the wounded fighters.

What foolishness! Let them fight to the death!

From behind Bom, a large Chihuahua barked at him.

"Bom! Bom!"

Bom didn't even turn, and give him the courtesy of his full attention. "What is it? Why do you bother me?"

The annoying Roog resembled a giant rat, and Bom had no patience with him.

"A cat has come aboard; says it has news of great importance. If you want Loki's female back..."

Bom spun on the daring intruder; cut him off with a throaty growl.

"My! Female!" he corrected. "My female!"

"It says," continued the other, undaunted. "He knows of her...wants to bargain."

"Where is it?"

"We hold it as prisoner in the lower decks."

"I will come," decided Bom.

The pesky dog-rat sped away, pleased with itself.

Probably nothing, but might as well investigate.

****

Spafford was shaking in his fur.

This was a stupid idea; what did I hope to accomplish?

But now, there was no avenue of escape left to him. And, he'd lose face if he backed down.

Is vengeance so important, that I am willing to join with the enemy?

Bom towered over him, smelling more fowl than usual; threatening.

"What do you want? Here among the Roog..."

"I am a Physician...here to offer my services," Spafford countered bravely. "Surely, the Roog have need of a Physician?"

"Those too badly injured to recover, we leave to die," Bom retorted coldly.

"I have news of the female from your prison; the one that went Noor," the Feline quickly interjected. "She is badly injured; hardly able to survive..."

"You tell me nothing, I did not already know. I am the one responsible; I did it to her," Bom boasted. "That's what you get for crossing me." He let the implied threat hang in the air.

Shocked and taken aback, Spafford had no words for the moment.

If Bom did that heinous act...and got away with it...why did he not finish the task?

The fact, Bom had threatened to harm him, failed to register on the Feline physician.

"Her males cannot heal her," ventured Spafford. "They seem to be powerless..."

"What was that?" Bom asked curtly, suddenly interested.

"The males have no powers. For that matter, all the Noor are so injured, and down, they can do little to even heal a small cut on their own bodies."

Chuckling, Bom sat down on his haunches next to the chained Feline.

"Tell me more."

"Loki is useless; can no longer take on the injury of another and instantly heal it. All he does is sleep beside the injured female. Liam is blind, or was when I left...none can teleport, not even Liam..."

Bom barked a laugh.

"And where are they hiding?"

"On Dia's ship, guarded by Feline only."

Bom pondered a moment, then asked the question most plaguing him.

"How did they escape the burial crypt I prepared for them?"

"As I heard it, the one called Tza was set free by a human..."

"I had him roped by the neck, tight against the wall; no way could he get free!"

"The story is, the little human found a knife, sawed him free..."

Bom growled angrily, as he realized his own stupidity.

"And now, Tza takes that human as his mate..."

If Spafford thought to incite a response toward the younger male, he was disappointed. Bom simply ignored the last remark, but he did appear provoked at Tza.

"Stupid, little, useless cat! I should have picked an older male...a warrior, to help with my cargo...not a young one with something to prove."

A silent pause ensued, as Bom thought through his options.

He finally turned on Spafford. "And, what do you hope to gain by this? I know your position on the ship was important. What made you leave it?"

"Liam forced me away..."

"Ah ha! You locked claws with the Noor leader, did you, now?"

Even Spafford knew his assumption was erroneous; Liam was no leader of any race. But he wasn't about to correct the Roog/Feline, and get himself killed. He was already in bed with the devil.

"What do you want of me?" growled Bom.

Trembling, but still determined, Spafford whined his request. "My freedom..." He held up his chained paws. "I will serve you...as your personal Physician," he warily suggested.

Once again, a silence followed, prolonged, nerve grating, and purposeful. Finally, Bom stood to his feet.

"Release this one," he ordered of those nearest. "He is not to be harmed further."

Chapter 23

She had been raped in the Roog prison breeder cells; then rescued by Uel, and finally, adopted into Dia's household, as the mate of the cherished guardian and friend to Loki.

Feather was human; Uel pure Feline, and the extended workers of Dia's nest were made up of many mixed species, yet all cuddled together in sleep upon the second mat provided by their employer, while Dia, her mate Kimon, and her Noor foster children were intertwined on the first.

But this night, most were unable to sleep, in fact all were tense and waiting. The birth time was well upon the Haida native, Feather; her water had broke many hours before.

Feather felt the deep agony of the driving ache. Though in labor most of the day, she had tried to hide the fact. In a clan full of Healers, even though many were suffering the pain of their own injuries, that had been a foolish endeavor. All knew what was happening. However, even the birthing mother was aware, because the Healers were all incapacitated, lacking their powers, they could not help. She was on her own.

Something is very wrong inside me. It feels like the baby is twisted, or caught up on something.

At her back, Uel cuddled against her, trying to give comfort, often moaning with her, as he felt her tense in a contraction, but totally helpless to assist in any significant way. In semi-darkness the two struggled unaided, while those about them emanated the emotion of sympathy. This nest was never uncompassionate.

Every agonizing throb; each excruciating building intensity, was felt by the empathic Healers around them, but the one who endured it most intensely was the broken, injured Noor, Susa...until she could stay idle no longer. Susa squirmed from beneath the arms of her Physical mate.

Feather was at the point of exhaustion; it was plain she would never deliver on her own.

Suddenly, Susa was next to them, pushing Uel out from his place, and moving in behind at Feather's back. The pain eased; taken by the Noor female.

Then Loki, too, was there, his large hands moving along the Haida's sides, and the pregnant one could feel, deep inside, the moving and turning of the infant. A twisted cord slipped from about the heel of the little one, there was a rush of liquid, and Feather, relieved greatly, slept...for a time.

Hours later, Feather hugged her new born against her breast, suckling it. Proud Uel, even though the babe was not of his own seed, nor Feline, but fully human, he had pledged to love and cherish her as his own.

After all, had he not been there, protecting it and its mother through all the long months before this tiny, delicate, helpless female was born? Besides, it was a female...a gift to be treasured.

Feather wonder at her blessings; most of all that the Instant Healers had come to her aid.

But how? I thought Susa was too injured to heal herself, let alone another.

At last, all in the nest slept, deeply and without pain.

****

It seemed, with that one unselfish act, the tides of healing were turned in the Noor's favor. As Susa and Loki healed back from helping in the delivery, the others of the clan made marvelous strides in their recovery, as well. Spirits rose, and laughter came again to Dia's nest.

Not only did all grow healthy, but in the weeks ahead, it was discovered, due to their sever torture and the following painful recovery, a new condition had developed in the females of immediate blood relationship to Susa. They had become exceedingly empathic, to the point of needing to alleviate suffering in another. Upon the thigh of each young female the heart Healer mark appeared, and as Susa and Loki guided them, their Instant Healer powers became extremely evident.

Loki and Susa now, were not the only Instant Healers. Moriah, Iora, and Kaudy were fast becoming proficient in this ability. Soon, their male partners learned their role, as well. Shiveron, the art of transferring his energy to Moriah; Reon to Iora, and Jabek to Kaudy. They learned to balance these females during the act of heal back, and quickly, reached the point where the males knew instantly if danger threaten any in their charge.

All this cemented the bond in the family; most times, it seemed, they were acting as one unit. Each in the Healer clan was aware instantly of the smallest threat to the others.

Soon, they took to the floor of the med facility, healing among the injured warriors, repairing severed limbs, broken bones, and twisted knees. Susa still bore some of the evidence of her brutal beating, yet no wounded warrior was repulsed by her face. They considered it a badge of beauty; as if she had been in battle with them.

Yes, for a time, Susa remained disfigured, her nose flattened, one cheek caved in, lips twisted. And the broken wing still hung useless behind her.

Chapter 24

One day Susa took Loki by the hand, and led her two males into the bath with her.

"I need your help. It is time to try to spread my wing."

"You sure?" Liam cautioned. "That won't be easy..."

"It needs doing," Susa decided. "And...it's beyond time to wake up the elders."

Liam raised an eyebrow, as if he knew exactly to what she referred.

"Witnesses?" he queried.

"Perhaps...Tia and Tza."

Liam quickly left the bath, returning shortly with the pair in tow.

"At no point are you to interfere," he instructed. "What happens in here, has never been seen by anyone other than a Noor. You have been given the privilege, because we feel you can be trusted, and we have need of someone in case this goes wrong. Tza, you will be guarding the entryway; let nothing distract you. We cannot afford someone entering unannounced."

Tza moved to a place just inside the sliding panels; they were already locked for safety, but both Kimon and Dia had the combination, and any other Noor could simply will it open. Obviously, the rest of the Noor family was excluded from this exercise.

"Tia, stay near him; in relaxed position, on your knees. Do not move from there, no matter what happens. We don't want you hurt. Should we not be successful in this, the Noor race will cease to exist. We will simply...vanish. If, after considerable time has passed, and we have not reappeared, notify Dia."

He then seemed to dismiss them, as if they were no longer present, and turned his attention fully on his junction and their mate.

****

"How do we go about this?" Liam asked of Susa.

"It is best we are all naked; the grip is stronger. Loki, you first. Kneel; I will sit in your lap, facing you. You must wrap your arms beneath my wings, behind me. Because you are the physical strongest, you must be the one to pull the hardest...when I give you the order."

Susa slipped gently onto the lap of her male Physical, but the action held no sensual arousal. Loki had steeled his reactions; he was ready. Each knew this exercise was not about love making.

"Now," Susa encouraged. "It's your turn, Liam. Come up behind my back; rest your head between my wings. Wrap your arms under my breasts...hard and tight, so as to brace me."

Preparing himself, as Susa had directed, Liam was aware, his function was not the most crucial. His main dread, was not that he would be inadequate, but what Loki, in fact, must do to their beloved.

"A word of caution," Susa continued. " I want both of you to promise...neither of you will try to absorb my pain."

"What?" challenged Loki. "Do you realize how excruciating this will be for you, if we don't?"

"Do what I ask, please. The point of this is for Tilk to be forced out...she needs to be the protector."

"Ah..." Both males understood now.

"Okay..." Susa sighed, as if reluctant to endure what was coming. "I am ready," she finally declared. "Pull hard...against each other...I...will...do...the rest."

While the males put all their strength behind their effort, Susa began to force, not only her good wing, but the one that had been severely maimed, broken, injured seemingly beyond repair, outward and up. Her face took on such a look of agony, it seemed, she must surely pass out.

The gossamer, butterfly-shaped wings slowly inched over and above Liam, hiding him. Their color, at first, was a light tan; then they appeared flecked with gold and silver. At last, the giant wings were of a turquoise and mauve appearance, with sparkling gold and silver flecks, jewel-like, still present.

Slowly, they inched out, until expanded to more than eight feet; twice the size of Susa's small body. Yet, still, one appendage appeared paralyzed, unable to stretch out completely to match with the other.

A cry of intense pain rend the silence.

It was not only heard, but felt in the minds of all on board the med ship. They knew, were conscious of great agony, yet unable to comprehend its origin. Until it passed, the crew of the ship held its collective breath, aware something beyond them was happening.

****

Suddenly, hovering over the Noor trio, was an image of such brightness, so harsh, it blinded those watching, so they had to turn away.

It was the mirror image of Susa; a creature of mere light; not of flesh at all, yet, so gorgeous...powerful. Tilk, the defender, had come out!

Liam slipped from the back of his mate, and with Loki, they dropped to one knee, facing Susa, on either side of her. All three were abruptly fully clothed, once again.

Slowly, Tilk descended, to stand and link hands with Susa.

Almost instantly, the stiff wing was healing, stretching with the other upward. The eyes of the blind one, became those of Tilk; wells of rainbow, whirling, color, sending forth evident power. Together with the Essence, Susa raised her fisted hands, also toward the sky. Shouting out in a commanding voice, she ordered:

"Awaken sleepers!"

The room filled with blinding light; the air seemed to crackle. Lightning flashed, though there were no clouds.

Small pin points of blue light appeared at every corner of the roof, grew larger, and became men and women. There were twelve in all; paired, each sex of equal number. These were unbelievably stunning of countenance; glowing; transparent; and when they spoke, the words resounded in your mind.

****

Afterward, Tia could never say directly, what she had seen...or heard, for that matter. She only knew what had been explained to her mind, after the fact:

Long ago, when Tilk, through intolerable torture, had lost her first physical counterpart, she realized the species would all die with her. Somehow, she had found the will and the energy; managing to separate twelve of her original people. Instantly, she had placed them in cryogenic suspension; sending them to the home planet; placing a sun-like protective field barrier about the home world, to prevent any that were not Noor from entering. The six couples had remained so, until this very day of their awakening.

It always puzzled Tia, and Tza too, why the Noor trio, when they had all this power at their disposal, went back to serve on the med floor of Dia's ship. After a silent conversation with the advanced Noor Elders, they sent them away; Tilk disappeared, and Liam, Loki and Susa returned to a semblance of servitude life. Susa again gave the appearance of one just recovered from a long battle with injury; the wings were hidden; the eyes though appearing to have healed, still seemed faulty; the body appeared to fatigue quickly; only a weak, frail individual.

Is this a cover to hide them? Or are they waiting for something; a time, perhaps, when the balance of influence would be just right?

The young couple knew that the Noor had this secret weapon, but they told no one. The younger of the Noor family seemed aware without being told; the Feline and the rest of the Universe, appeared clueless.

Chapter 25

Through the corridors of Dia's med ship crept one of the enemy. His purpose was not to eliminate, but to get to the communication center, where he would place a recorded message, and escape. As a spy, he was expendable, but Bom awaited confirmation that the deed was accomplished, so he needed to return, or he would forfeit his life, anyway.

Oblivious to the danger, Dia and her extended Noor family were just beginning their sleep break, and indulging in a meal prepared from scratch. It was the males' turn to cook, and Loki was most exuberantly enjoying the process, as he had been appointed sampler. They had just sat down to begin the meal.

Suddenly, over every speaker, ship-wide, the grating voice of the Roog/Feline, Bom, assaulted the senses of everyone present.

"We have your ship surrounded," Bom's commanding tones declared. "I will spare all others, if you give me what is mine: the one with my tattoo on her hand; the blue butterfly! She must come to me alone, without her protective males. None other may accompany her. If they do, they will forfeit their lives."

All hands at the meal stopped in mid-purpose; all eyes went searchingly to Susa. Loki bristled; Liam growled at the audacity of the giant Roog/Feline.

As the message repeated, all realized their security had been breached again; it was a recording placed in the system. Immediately, Liam sent out feelers to count the casualties. There were none, which meant someone had been lax.

"I have prepared a connecting corridor directly to my warship," continued the insistent voice. "I am patient, but I will only wait mere hours. Then you will all visit my dungeons, and pay with your lives."

Reports were coming back from the warrior stations around the ship. These confirmed what Bom had spoken; they were indeed surrounded, with a ship to ship passageway connecting to one of the ships.

"What do you want us to do?" Steven demanded. "We're willing, whatever that may be."

Liam didn't have a chance to answer; Susa's quiet voice broke into the silence.

"I will go to him. It is time for this to end."

****

All Dia's extended, and family, stood watching the nest monitor. The Noor members knew they were not at the mercy of Bom, but the Feline, and other members, expected the worst.

"She looks so helpless," Feather observed, as she cuddled her newborn close in trepidation. "And...alone."

Liam made a movement with his hand, and the picture above change to one of infrareds; suddenly they could see the invisible. Around the calf of her left leg, Susa was wearing, what appeared to be, a small snake anklet.

"Holy!" exclaimed Steven jubilantly. "Oona is with her! I thought he said, none may accompany her?"

"I believe his meaning was a warm blooded being..." Liam defended. "Oona is neither warm, nor cold..."

A chuckle ran through the observers, and hope was kindled in their chests.

****

The personal of both ships watched her progress on monitors; but the shocked warriors of her vessel suddenly became aware, things were not as they appeared. Her shape-shifter nature gave Susa the ability to camouflage and disguise. If she could do that, what else was possible? Hope rose to new heights.

Her braces were back; she staggered and limped. Her skin color was pallid, almost grey. The tiny bit of fur visible on her back, above her shirt collar, was a sickly yellow, instead of the usual white sheen.

Her tail, missing sections of the fur, was limp and matted. Worse was her face: she appeared blind; one eye turning in toward the nose; both lids half closed. And behind her back, hung one stunted wing, broken and useless, while the other was not apparent at all. A bed-draggled, defeated-appearing individual by all manifestation.

Susa tread the long coil-like corridor slowly, dragging her tail for effect. It was her intention, to appear as helpless as possible, so Bom remained off guard, as long as achievable. She needed to be up close before they could strike.

When she finally entered the large room, Bom stood with his followers, waiting. He towered above her, slavering with anticipation, his claws extending and retracting nervously.

"Ah," he mourned, with feigned sympathy. "The little she is hurt. How do you suppose that happened?" He laughed derisively, and his henchmen joined in. "So unfortunate...perhaps, she won't fight me so hard this time?"

His voice held a note of regret, almost as if he had anticipated a chase before the kill.

"Come closer," Bom ordered curtly. " Not so pretty anymore, eh? Nose squashed. Aw...can't heal that wing?" he probed.

Susa said nothing. She had left the scars of the beating visible purposely, that he might witness how she had to struggle back from the brink. Now, she stepped closer, within his shadow; she made no effort to change her appearance.

Off to the side, she was aware of one who shouldn't be there at all. The traitor, Spafford, was flanked on all sides by the larger Roog. He seemed defiant, yet a little uncertain, as well.

"This fight is between you and me," offered Bom, as he noted her head had turned toward the crowd around them. "The others will be mere spectators. They will not interfere!"

He said that last in louder tones, as if it were an order he expected followed.

Susa growled deep in her throat.

Enough of this!

****

He never noticed the rapid change in her. Bom was so huge, compared to the half-sized Noor female, he perceived only slowly what took place at his feet. By then, it was already too late.

The large muscled back leg of the giant brushed by Susa's small left foot.

This beast threatens the life of the mistress! My life for his!

In a flash, quicker than the eye could see, Oona materialized, and became a living, deadly weapon. She struck the killer blow, even before she had fully changed, or even was visible.

Venom coursed up the leg of the huge aggressor, up to the heart, paralyzing...but not lethal, after all. Of course, such a tiny Slither could not kill one so large, but the baby gave it her all.

Bom went down, heavily hitting the deck; on his back, paws limp and useless by his sides, tongue lolling, droll already evident, he lay there unable to move.

The verification of the torturer, powerless, at long last before them, did something to Susa's control. Tilk, the protector, the aggressor, the avenger, took the upper hand; Susa no longer had the say. Tilk had waited too long for this!

Using the body of Susa as her physical weapon, Tilk pounced on the prostrate form of Bom. Giving way to pent up anger, and the extreme wrath of ages, she bared the teeth, and with claws extended, dug into the flesh of her tormentor.

She hovered for a second, as if her second half was upbraiding her, demanding she stop, and refusing, raked her claws across the beastly face. The paralyzed predator could do nothing, though he was awake to see what was coming.

****

Behind the monitor, Loki growled low in his throat, in full agreement with what was taking place.

"Now," he admitted, viciously. "Wouldn't I like to join her at that."

"Go for it," Liam seconded, as vengeful of spirit, as his counterpart.

****

Instantly, Loki stood beside Susa. His anger brought her to her senses.

With a sob, at the realization of what she had just done; blood dripping from her jaws, she withdrew from her victim. She crouched over Bom, regret bombarding her soul, yet she hovered over his face, snarling for effect, and watched the fear in the eyes of the vulnerable coward.

I could have torn him to ribbons...

At the change in his mate, Loki suddenly sobered. Tongue in cheek, calm as you please, placidly, he offered:

"Need some help?"

Susa turned her head, apology in her eyes.

"Later...you may help me heal...the damage I have done..."

Surprise mirrored in the victim's eyes.

Loki chuckled.

"He is reluctant to believe, we could be more benevolent than he, now that we have him cornered."

And finally, Loki got a smile from his beloved. She stood up; the blood disappeared from her face.

"Liam, come!" she ordered.

Obediently, the Mental junction appeared on the other side of Bom.

"Shackle him," Susa commanded.

Chains appeared; wrapping quickly around ankles, to pull up, and encase the paws, behind the back, as without his will, Bom was rolled to his side.

Once again, surprise was evident in the eyes of the captured one.

Liam grinned.

"Thought we had no powers, didn't you, Bom? Yes, we lost them for a time, but we are back full force, and you won't easily thwart us again. Your day is done. Take a look around you."

The Roog/Feline's eyes went to the circle of his males. They seemed to have moved back, as if held behind some sort of barrier. None had made, even an effort, to go to his aid.

It was then Bom became aware of the sentinel bright lights near the ceiling above; there were also six along the invisible obstruction which held his followers at bay.

Susa's voice interrupted his reverie.

"Imprison them all," she commanded. "Even Spafford."

The Feline physician turned to look at her fearfully, and began to whine.

"You had your chance, male," Susa declared. "And...you chose the wrong side."

Turning away, completely dismissing the other prisoners, and those who came to help cart them away to the cell block, Susa quietly, in a tone of regret and remorse, asked her Physical to aid her.

"Loki...please...help me heal away these injuries I have inflicted."

Dropping to one knee beside Bom, Loki joined hands with the Noor female.

Chapter 26

Clio was a proud Roog leader; no one in his right mind would cross him, and live to tell the tale. The male was just as certain of his station, as the ruler of the Universal Council.

In his twisted way of thinking, he prided himself on an unbiased ability to oversee them.

Mind you, it was just as possible, he could be against a ruling, ruler, or race, as he was to agree with them, though he was not supposed to take sides; merely to pass judgment on the ruling of the others.

An overseer, the chair of the council, was theoretically neutral.

Today, as one of the leading prominent races represented, and also that administrator, Clio took his seat at the center of the half ring of twelve seats. This day, the others had the voting power, but he planned to have the final say. He also meant to make a quick end of this charade; an end that favored his son. He would let this farce of a trial go on just so long; then he would end it.

How dare this upstart Noor female accuse Bom of any crime!

Yes, his uninhibited offspring showed his fight sometimes, but to accuse his son of misdeeds was a slight to the blood line of Clio, and the Roog leader would have none of it.

The little she, appearing frail and unsteady, stood with her representative in the docket. Half the size of Bom, yet it was rumored, she had singlehandedly bested him.

She should be the one on trial here! How dare she!

Clio hadn't bothered to view the evidence. Should he have his way, those hologram projections would be declared inadmissible. But he was determined, this would be stopped, before they reached that point.

"The chair is of the opinion, that this grievance is not a case at all. I fail to acknowledge it, on the grounds that a female cannot be a victim, as by Roog law and rules, all such creatures are but property, and therefore have no rights. The one, Bom, has not offended, as these incidents occurred among the Roog. Case rejected! And dismissed."

"When the Roog joined the Universal federation," objected counsel for the plaintive. "They agreed to follow Universal rules. The prisoner is being tried under those laws. Also, as the occurrences cover more than one time frame, and were perpetrated against the ruler of another species, it involves the laws of that race, as well."

Clio growled with annoyance. "To what species do you refer?"

"The Noor species, sir."

Clio made a sound that was meant to be a rough, derisive laugh, but it came out as a bark of arrogant disgust, instead.

"The Noor race has been exterminated; it is extinct! And, the halves, are but a plague, that needs to be eradicated."

The Feline lawyer, on the plaintive podium, turned to plead with the decision making members of the board.

"Council members, we appeal to your judgment. It is obvious our neutral judge is biased. We request that he be removed, and another, with a more impartial mindset, be installed in his stead."

"You have no power to make such an appeal," stated Clio vehemently. "Request denied!"

But the lawyer persisted. "I did not yet wish to play this card," he declared. "But, my course has been forced. From evidence viewed pretrial, we have concluded that the mighty Roog leader is also an accomplice, implicated in the crimes of his son, Bom...therefore, we ask that Clio be placed in custody, to be tried immediately, alongside his son."

Clio sputtered with sudden indignation, yet it did him no good. He instantly found himself in a shielded prisoner box similar to that which housed his son.

What is this? Are the Noor back to controlling us?

****

The expressionless voice of the mechanical intoned: "Dia of the Feline race has been chosen as substitute overseer. Please, take your place, so the proceedings may continue."

When Dia was in position, the mechanical read the charges:

"Prisoner #1: representing the Roog nation; Clio, you are charged with ordering the destruction of the Noor leadership, and with the death of their ruler, destroying the species. How do you plead?"

Clio by passed his appointed counsel, shouting from the prisoner's box:

"I had nothing to do with this; I am falsely accused!"

"We put forth the plea of 'not guilty!'" the Roog lawyer, representing his leader, proclaimed, vehemently. "And ask that this trial be declared a sham."

"Motion denied!" Dia declared. "I have viewed the evidence, and there is sufficient for the case to proceed."

Once again, the mechanical read charges: "Prisoner #2: Bom, cross-breed of Feline and Roog races; you are charged with ending the physical life of a Noor Leader Female, and imprisoning her Essence. Second charge: the beating of one Susa, the second chosen Physical of the ruler and holder of the Noor peoples, the Essence, Tilk; and attempting the destruction of said Physical. Third charge: confining an intelligent human species, treating them as cattle, and using them for the purpose as a food source, and thereby, causing the destruction of said peoples. How do you plead?"

For a moment, the counselor for Bom stood slack jawed in astonishment; as if he had been unaware of the extent of the heinous deeds of his client. In the prisoner's box, Bom merely sneered.

At last, the Lawyer entered the plea of 'not guilty on all counts'."

The mechanical again intoned: "Prisoner #3: Spafford, Physician of the Feline race; you are charged with Treason. How do you plead?"

The Feline lawyer was the only one to say: 'guilty as charged'."

Then, the prosecution went in to its presentation.

****

"To substantiate first charge of Prisoner #1: from the memory stream of one Tilk, we present the actions, as they took place. These have been verified, by also scanning the recollections of Clio and Bom, though the last were taken by force, and against their will."

"Objection!" shouted the counselors for Clio and Bom in unison.

"The rights of the prisoner have been violated!" added Clio's representative. "Does he have no respect as Leader of the Roog?"

Dia allowed a silence to hang in the air, as if she were deliberating that very question. When at last she spoke, it was not the answer the dog creatures expected.

"The Roog have been at war with many creatures; Is this not a common fact?" She did not wait for an answer. "When you joined our federation, you agreed to follow our guidelines. One was to cease war on the member races of the council, which we have noted, your Leader has failed to enforce. As he had no respect for prior promises agreed upon, I fail to see why Clio deserves the deference of this judicial body. However...we note your objection; but...as it is the procedure in such cases, memory gathering is not a practice of which you may find fault. Objection over ruled!"

Then addressing the plaintive counsel, Dia added: "Please, continue."

As a holographic projection suspended in mid air, a vision-like scene appeared before the court. The time period was in the distant past; long before many present were born.

The scene revealed a stunningly beautiful humanoid female, imprisoned in a drain-belt. It was obvious she was Noor, for though they were extremely battered, behind her back, a pair of butterfly-like wings hung limp, and quite visible. All viewing, immediately became aware, this woman was the Noor ruler, for only she had sported such appendages.

Surrounded by Roog much larger than she, the helpless creature lay on the ground, her belly extended. Obviously giving birth, she was in the final throes of delivery, for the unfortunate child had already come forth; one lower limb free; the other caught inside the mother.

As the imprisoned Queen turned her head, the court was given a view of a much younger Clio, standing off to the side, with Bom, who was then no more than a five foot tall pup. According to the time line, displayed above the images, Clio had just admitted to the fathering of this male, and had taken him under his tutelage.

"This shall be your challenge," Clio informed his new found son. "Your task is to kill this she, and her half-born trash. Show me you are more Roog than cat, for you seem, weakling; their cowardice has rubbed off on you."

Bom growled rejection of the statement, and howled in anger. "I am Roog!"

"Then make me a proud father!" goaded Clio.

He handed the younger male a heavy metal bar.

Bom stepped forward, his features distorted by hate, yet underneath timidity and hesitancy warred for the upper hand. His fear was great of this creature that had fathered him, and he would do anything to remain in his good graces.

Standing over the vulnerable Noor female, for a second, Bom appeared to have empathy with her, but it was short lived, replaced by an evident feeling of power, and enjoyment of the task, that was obviously, an unadulterated Roog trait.

With all the force he could muster, Bom laid the first blow. In rapid succession, each blow that followed, did more damage, than that which came before, until both the new born child, and its mother were nothing but gasping pulp.

The older female struggled to move her infant to her arms.

Clio did not order cessation; nor did Bom quit, until he himself was spent. It was when he stopped to rest, incredibly, the battered being rose up with her infant in her arms...and vanished.

The memory faded out; came back to another similar scene. Something had been skipped. Now the mother was alone...perhaps, she had not wanted the court to see the death throes of her child?

No one could blame her.

All watched, as Tilk's first Physical expired...the Essence floated.

Growls and howls of appreciation exploded from the Roog surrounding the prisoner, but the one from whom Bom had hoped to gain accolades, merely ignored him; turned to the appreciative crowd, and raised his paw for silence.

"Tonight we feast on Noor meat. It is my gift to you. But...we are not finished. The Essence is immerging. Confine it!"

Then what was left of Tilk was incased in a box, surrounded by vacuum. They had thought they could contain it.

****

In the prisoner's box, Clio sneered. He remembered all too well. He took a moment to relive the thrill of his greatest triumphant, the recapture of the escaped Noor female. And, even to this day, there was no repentance in his spirit...just an all consuming wrath toward anything Noor.

That time had also been his greatest defeat! The feast had been the deadliest ever indulged in by the Roog. The Noor's flesh was poison to all who ate of it that night.

Perhaps, I should have let Bom partake? But...if I hadn't been punishing him, for allowing the She to go free, I too would have been at the feasting...we both would now be dead...we wouldn't be in this present predicament, and...I would be rid of him!

Clio scowled at where his thoughts were going. He growled, and spat, as if the memory brought a bad taste to his mouth. Those watching, shivered, and were glad he was confined.

****

The memory blinked off. Over the court room fell a deadly hush, broken at last by the grating tones of the mechanical court secretary.

"How votes the council?"

As one, the verdict was unanimous: "The evidence speaks for itself. Most certainly...guilty!"

"The defendant will remain until sentence is determined."

Chapter 27

"The trial for second prisoner will now commence: as to the first indictment: it is evident from the previous trial, who held the weapon that killed. This court, by prior agreement, considers the judgment for Clio, binding also for Bom, so there is no need to rehash. Therefore we go on to second charge: to substantiate that accusation, we take from the memory of one Loki, present through the encounter, and witness to the fact; again, we verify from Bom's own recollections."

As with the first, the vision-like memory appeared before the court: The metal bar fell; it injured; created excessive damage. The crunch of bone was clearly heard, as it smashed in the face; shattered the leg and arm, cracked the vertebrae of the spine, broke the delicate wing. The liquid sound of blood spatter, as it hit the stone floor, could almost be smelled, as well as perceived, by the audience of millions.

All across the Universe, on every planet of the civilized system, at multiple view stations, the eyes of the federated planets watched this trial. Those who had been wronged by Bom, falsely imprisoned by him; lost loved ones to the Roog, all waited to see this obnoxious warden get his due. It had been a long time in coming.

As the ugly, ill-smelling, giant beast lounged in his shielded cage, unconcerned, there was none who would have voted in his favor. He had not drawn much goodwill toward his deeds; nor did he much care.

When the memory of Loki played for all, and each watched the terrible unprovoked beating of Susa, the helpless rage of the Noor Physical came through, as well.

"Why did he not stop Bom?" one watcher wondered of another.

"Can you not see the chains wrapped around him; the drain-belt at his waist?" offered his companion. "He's rendered weak and helpless..."

"And," offered a third. "He's in that small metal cage; can't even move...so tiny to fit a giant like him..."

And so, when the beings watched, many not only sympathized with the beaten victim, but remembered numerous such blows, and confinement of their own. The anger that came through from Loki was not his alone. It was shared by the many left behind, when Bom had done like deeds to their families: killed a mother, a daughter, son, or father. All across the unified Universe, the judgment was already passed; Pity and empathy was abundant toward both Susa and Loki.

And so, when the verdict was spoken, it was cheered across open space, resounding from planet to planet.

As the memories faded from view, Dia asked:

"How do the members vote?"

Once more, the results were unanimous: "Guilty, beyond doubt!"

The observation of a witness was never disputed.

Yet, there was one more charge to contend with. Those of human origin, both recently rescued, and from older established colonies, waited and watched with bated breath.

Chapter 28

"Regarding charge #3: confining an intelligent human species, treating them as cattle, and using them for the purpose of a food source, and thereby, causing the destruction of said peoples.

"Memory stream is from one, Uel: a Feline, who spent his years from seven to adulthood in the prison establishment of Bom. He now serves as Physician on the med-ship of Dia, and is considered reliable. Verified by the memories of others such as: Loki; Liam, and Bom. As these verifying streams are from opposing sides, no objection will be permitted."

The memory was mostly that of Uel, beginning by showing a very young Feline, incarcerated because Bom falsely accused him of stealing. When Uel first entered the underground prison, many of the Universe, from word of mouth, were familiar with it. All their lives, they had dreaded being sent there, but most had disbelieved the stories told...until now. Sympathy was quickly on Uel's side.

Even at this early date, Bom had his human food system set up. As the viewers followed the imprisoned youth through his appointed, scheduled work routine, those witnessing experienced the filth of the holding pens reserved for those labeled 'meat'; the crowded 'breeder' cells, where the women fought for every morsel of food they ingested; the unorthodox breeding practices, and lastly, as Uel was assigned as hospital orderly, the delivery, and disposal practices.

Angry cries, from the throats of their peoples, were heard on every human planet in the far reaches of the unified system. Not only from them, but from every species viewing, came indignant and horrified comments at what they saw. Outraged calls were coming in at the switch boards on many of the ships guarding the Judicial Council, the trial, and the prisoners; each demanding more than instant death as punishment; a more appropriate, justifiable retribution; the sentence of torture for life.

This was no longer viewed with interested detachment; no longer simply a case of a Noor being violated. It was now personal! Human kind was involved; Feline and other races that had struggled with Roog atrocities. A cry for retribution, unlike any other, spread from solar sun to solar system.

"How does the council vote?" demanded the mechanical.

And from each came: "Guilty!"

Chapter 29

It was finally time for the sentencing. The humans in the far flung planets held their breath. They, and many others, expected a bloodletting, but how could that be adequately executed?

What was eventually put forth, and enacted, both surprised...and pleased, the majority, for its appropriateness.

****

Dia spoke humbly, in the silence after the audience had been shushed; the cheers had finally died away.

"Clio and Bom, you have been tried, and convicted; found guilty on all counts. Punishment is for the neutral chair to decide. However, as I feel I am too personally, and emotionally involved, it is my duty to relinquished the task to another.

"We have decided to invoke an old forgotten law, which allows the victim to chose...and enforce...punishment. In the opinion of the court, it seems, that because she is both human and Noor, and has been the most grievously wronged, Tilk/Susa should perform this duty.

"How say you, Noor Queen: what shall these two do to make restitution for their crimes?"

Susa's voice was quiet, but clear.

"The harm done to the Noor species can never be compensated. It was irreparably damaged by the death of our first Physical. As for my personal discomfort, I, Susa, count that as not.

"It is my opinion, that no penalty will change the behavior of either of these males, nor will they cease to offend, if left as they are, but...I will decide their fate...and enforce it, as the court wishes."

"Then come forward and do so," Dia instructed.

From the box of the plaintive, a small form moved across the floor of the huge chamber. At center stage, she stood between the three prisoner cages, and the ruling judicial body, seated around the horse-shoe shaped table. The sudden surprise appearance of her two giant, guardian males, one on either side of her, brought a shocked gasp from those present.

Even more so, was the astonishment, when the bright manifestation of blue Noor elders appeared along the roof line of the stadium. Many were filled with dread and awe, for from stories of old, they knew these were very powerful, and until now, had assumed all their influence had been lost.

"First," Susa proclaimed timidly. "As Leader, appointed by Kei, of the Feline species, I would like to address the crime of the one who wronged that peoples. Spafford: you pled guilty to your charge of Treason, and therefore, though Feline law demands the death penalty, I will be lenient on you. You chose to take sides against your own race; supplying information to the enemy, which lead Bom to your new ruler. Because you used your tongue to betray, you will be rendered deaf, and mute, and will remain so, until your dying day. As you also distained the station of Physician, your duties, from this moment on, will be to serve obediently, with no higher rank than a mere mechanical; cleaning, cooking, and providing for those of the profession you abandoned. I place only one stipulation upon this sentence: you may serve only on another med-ship other than that of Dia."

The prisoner, Spafford covered his head in his shame, and wondered if his sentence was really more benevolent than death.

"I will now seek to pronounce appropriate retribution for the crimes of Bom: Half-one: many times you have voiced this slur in the face of my family, but are we so different? You also are of more than one species...the only divergence is that your father's race was malevolent, while those from whom we came, were the opposite.

"I address the last charge only: you have taken many human lives, and no amount of retaliation, or torment, will bring them back to life. Besides, my Noor belief tells me, vengeance is not mine to seek. The Almighty Creator will do that for us. So, in keeping with His mercy, in my spirit, I forgive you..."

Until now, Bom had sat defiant, his arms folded across his chest. Now he barred his teeth viciously, growled furiously, and with claws extended, rose up to his full height. He jarred the barrier of his surroundings, with a powerful shoulder, over and over, in his anger, but to no avail.

"I...we, forgive you, but...there is still the matter of retribution, which is demanded by this court, and others...you must be punished appropriately.

"You have used your intelligence to devise misery; your size to dominate, and inflict cruelties. Both will be taken from you, but...you shall retain your memories. You despised your mother's people, so...you will live as a small kitten, no bigger than the palm of my hand. You will take the form of a helpless, maimed creature who has been brutalized, with claws and fangs removed. Your fur will have been scorched; your tail clipped short. Without assistance, you cannot even feed yourself, leave alone, survive.

"A human will find you, and take pity on you. The benevolent being will be but a child; she will take care of you diligently, with kindness. You will outlive her; and another will take her place. You will live long. Each time your human pets you; feeds, and cares for you, you will remember what you did to others like her.

"What I have decreed will begin now! This second, Bom, you will be found in the alley of a human colony city. Remember...I forgive you."

And Bom vanished from the prisoner's box, never to be seen again.

****

The hushed courtroom took a moment to recover, but Susa went on, as if in a hurry to be done with the fowl deeds.

"I will next sentence, Clio, ruler of the Roog peoples...and with him, his species," Susa proclaimed; no malice evident in her tone.

"It is my opinion," the Noor Leader admitted sadly. "That as long as there is a Roog in the Universe, the beings in it will always be their prey. As this species took part in both my capture, the death of the preceding Physical attached to Tilk, and the industry of human breeding and consumption, they must be included in this judgment. From this moment on, forever, all Roog will be reduced in intelligence, unable to converse verbally; they shall never grow bigger than two feet tall.

"Throughout the coming days, they will be herded, without mercy, into cages, and sold to the human colonies, some as meat to Chinese customers, others as pets for children; forever helpless, no longer a danger to those around them."

Susa paused for effect.

"Clio: you mean nothing to me! Your fate will be the same as that of your people, with the exception of this: unlike your populace, who will remember none of this, you will retain the knowledge of the glory you once had, and unwisely, threw away. As the pet of a human child, you will serve every whim of your tiny master, savor it, and long for his approval. You will have no voice by which to counsel; watch the boy make his mistakes, and be hurt by them, unable to prevent or succor."

As Susa turned from Clio, both he and his counselor shrank to a mere two feet tall. Their unintelligent barking did not hide their frustration.

Susa then addressed the Judicial body: "I have done what was required; if it please the court, I will now take my leave."

She did not need their permission, nor did she see the consenting nods. When Tilk/Susa vanished with her Junction males, not only were the trials over, but also, the Noor had, in fact, facilitated the end of the Roog/Feline war.

Chapter 30

To celebrate the removal of the enemy threat, the next day Dia proclaimed a holiday, for all the living aboard her ship. And as everyone was free from duty, which had been left in the hands of mechanical staff, the ship owner took her family, and those attached to her nest, on a tour of the scenic areas of her gigantic transport.

Along the exercise track, where, for the first time since her battered form had been brought aboard, Susa beat Loki at a race; through the hydroponics gardens; and on into the parks of fruit trees and flowers, the troupe followed after the Feline matriarch. Susa, Liam and Loki, were as but children once again, following the leadership of a Feline foster mother much smaller than most of her adopted kits.

Strung out behind the Noor, and intermingled with them were those of Human, Feline, Bear, and Slither peoples, that guarded, or served, and were protected by the family.

Twila and Nyle were walking with Tia and Tza at the back of the line, taking their time sightseeing, but the conversation had turned to Tilk/Susa...and what had happened at the trial.

"It seems so unbelievable that a human could have developed such stupendous powers," remarked Tia. "Is it possible for all humans to reach that accomplishment?"

Twila gave a purring laugh. "Susa has very little human in her..."

"But didn't she begin as a human?" challenged Tia.

Nyle chuckled. "I have a question for you. By now, you are familiar with our whole story; even mine. When I went through my evaluation on Jump Station, and was found compatible to Twila, at that time, they already said I had the Noor blood anomaly...that was even before Loki transfused my mom. How could that be?"

Perplexed, both Tia and Tza shook their heads.

"You haven't figured it out yet?" encouraged Nyle. "Here is another question: what happened in the break between the segments of Tilk's memory stream? Use your imagination."

For a moment Tia pondered, frowning.

"What happened to that baby?" Tia exclaimed. "Maybe, it didn't die? Where did Tilk go? What did she do?"

"Ha! Now you're getting it," Nyle said in approval.

"Tilk caused the break in the memory stream, deliberately," Twila supplied. "She didn't want the whole Universe knowing she got away from her captors long enough to hide her baby."

"She was recaptured?"

"No," Twila admitted. "She left the baby on the steps of a human orphanage. Then to keep the Roog from tracing the infant, she intentionally backtracked to meet her tormentors, and sacrificed herself, by being recaptured again. Remember, she was still in a drain-belt, and couldn't escape Earth. During her free time, she had also put some of the elders in stasis..."

"But...why didn't she send the baby with them?"

"The infant was too badly injured; all Tilk could manage was to turn her completely human, but...that didn't remove the Noor blood from her veins. It stayed dormant through all these years."

"Then...Susa is that baby?" asked Tza in astonishment.

"Oh, no," Nyle countered. "But close."

"The generation difference is too long," Twila revealed. "A dormant Noor can't live as long, as we normally do. The baby grew up on the Forbidden Planet, married, had children..."

"We all were born dormant, so to speak," Nyle admitted. "But though we appeared human, we were only part...undiscovered..."

"Until?"

"Until my mom nearly died in Bom's prison."

"Oh, geeze!" Tia exclaimed. "Tilk is Susa's ancestor!"

"No wonder!" marveled Tza. "Tilk, chose to bond with her."

Nyle grinned. "The Almighty Creator had it planned from the beginning."

"So," Tia reluctantly admitted, after a time. "I guess humans can't be that mentally powerful...after all."

"Tilk is the power behind them. She had centuries to develop and hone her talents."

"You'd think your Almighty Creator would never let someone so potent exist, without challenge," suggested Tia.

Twila giggled. "Who says the Creator never tests us? What just happened? Eh?"

Epilogue:

When the invitation went out, many were thrilled at the prospect of seeing her, especially those of Feline and Human persuasion. The double Queen for the Noor, and Feline, was about to make an announcement which would impact both species. All were encouraged to attend if they could make it to Jump Central grand auditorium. If not, viewer screens would be available on all planets.

Most of those rescued from the Forbidden Planet were still on the Jump Station, being processed. They had a ringside seat; mind you, what was announced proved not exactly to their liking.

****

For the presentation, Susa wanted a vehicle that would serve two purposes: one; to act as a carrier, as they sped across space to their destination; the second; to serve as protection on site. Its final function would be to present the family, and their extended staff, as a unified, and well-guarded entity.

The Universal Leader knew, she could protect herself, and if she couldn't, her Junction males, and Elders, were a mighty guardian force. Now that the Roog had been dealt with, as far as the Felines were concerned, they were quite confident, their new appointed Queen was secure. But Tilk/Susa was aware of other factors; that as long as they were on public display, she and her family, being Noor, would never be safe. There were always those who would experiment with Roog toys; plans were still in circulation for the drain-belts, and the deadly drain-beam...

In her mind, Susa also had an ulterior reasoning for building the transport. It was her intention, when she was done with it, to pass it on to Dia and Kimon. They, and their future Feline guardian warriors, would have need of it later.

Never again would the Noor Queen leave her family unguarded. Her first duty was to protect the Noor peoples! Therefore, it was intended that every Noor-half in the clan, and all extended personal, would accompany her, when, as the Feline/Noor Universal Council Head, she presented the decisions made, to her subjects.

It was agreed, in order to keep the Humans; Felines; young adults and infants, safe, the shielding of the craft must first be armor plated. This would deflect all rays, whether from mere radiation, or the lethal drain-beam, used against the Noor.

It was Thor, Nyle, and Steven, who set to work developing such an all purpose ship.

****

The vehicle, that materialized at the very center of the stadium, was boat-shaped, covered completely by a metallic silver casing. Upon arrival, it powered down, and the top shielding slowly lowered half way, revealing an upper dome of transparent Plexiglas.

At the very front, driving the carrier, was the Feline, Tzachok; his beautiful long-haired white coat was spotless, as he proudly sat at the controls. Directly behind him, and a step below, was his chosen human mate, Tia, ready at the secondary board, just in case something happened to Tza. Her long reddish-black hair fell straight down her back to her hips; her flawless bronzed skin, and slanted eyes, denoted her Japanese heritage.

Tilk/Susa had insisted, no female, or other attendant staff, be less protected than the actual core Noor group, and so, all partners were aboard; the females on the inner side, on a platform a step lower than the males.

As extra protection, all along the outer side edges of the craft, the warrior members of the clan were placed. Each female partner was beside her male; one step lower to ensure added shelter. Down the right side, going toward the back, were stationed: Thor, with Reva; the Slither pair, Sith, and Serene. At the immediate rear of the transport, was Steven, with Amara. Along the left side, going forward, was the Bear couple, Wadi, with Rimu, and just ahead of them, was Uel. Inside and below him, was Feather Cloud, dressed clearly in Haida garments to proclaim her aboriginal heritage; cradling her new born infant in her arms.

There was a second circle inside the guardians shielding, formed by the Noor family. Here again, you found the females on the inside, and the next shelf lower. Right to left was: Shiveron, with Moriah; then Reon, with Iora, her tight black curls re-grown, down her back; her caramel skin evidence of her black human birthright. At the back were Jabek and Kaudy. While on the left, Nyle stood alone, with Twila on the inside.

The inner portion of the craft appeared empty. All anyone could see, just back of the pilots, was the Feline, Dia, heavy with kit, and her Physician mate, Kimon. In the matriarch's arms was a female human child of approximately two; Ta-Ta, guarded possessively for Amara, by the owner of the med-ship.

A stillness of expectation over hung the building. Then, an expansive, circular platform began to rise up slowly, from the vacant center of the vehicle.

Again there was a pause, heightening the anticipation. Yet, the first to appear was not the expected celebrity, but a gigantic Noor/Feline male with his arms crossed defiantly over his chest.

The size of this being so shocked those watching, a collective gasp escaped from the crowd. He was enormous, colossal, and massive. He stood close to nine feet tall;

weighed at least six hundred pounds, with a topnotch of curls of red/gold sprinkled with silver/black. His eyes were those of a Feline; turquoise with a bronze vertical slit center. The face, hands, and feet were humanoid, but the ears, and ten foot shorthaired tail, behind him, was purely Feline.

It was obvious to those watching, this creature was meant to intimidate; to produce the effect, that he protected the Universal Queen. They assumed it was all for showmanship; none realized, that was the Junction's actual form.

To the astonishment of the audience, he suddenly became two. One male was now clearly ginger haired, while the second, on the right, sported a topnotch of black streaked with silver. Each had shrunk slightly in size, approximately a foot, but the one on the left was clearly heavier, and more physically powerful than the other. The darker haired one wore a tight fitting jumpsuit of mauve; while the golden haired one was clothed in blue. From the trial, it was recognized, this was apparently, Loki.

A cheer went up at this realization.

The two stepped apart. A second smaller platform rose from the center, to a position above the knees of the males.

A silence fell over the crowd, as they realized, what they had come for, was finally happening.

Leisurely, the figure of Tilk/Susa materialized. But to the crowd, next to her gigantic partners, she seemed a displeasure.

At first, she appeared but a miniature version of the males; though clearly female, with her short silver/white curls, the cat tail, and the humanoid face and hands, she appeared a tiny, defenseless, powerless, disappointment. Her only ornaments were a silver band around her forehead, dangling butterfly earrings, and a snake-like anklet around her left calf. She wore a simple gold dress, with a short pleated skirt.

Most were disenchanted mainly, because they had expected her to look more impressive, and superior, to the males.

Just goes to caution you; never judge by the parcel packaging the person.

****

Her massive eight foot wings spread out behind her gradually. They were like those of a butterfly, the color of turquoise with mauve markings, speckled by gold and silver. As they extended, she raised her fisted hands to the rafters, thrilling her audience, as they witnessed the phenomena of the blue light Elders' sudden appearance at the corners of the roof.

All assumed, now, her protectors had arrived, and these were the source of her power. But, they were wrong; these Seniors' endowment came through her; not the other way around.

Knowing their misconceptions, reading idol worship in their thoughts, Susa began her words with humility in her tone.

****

The audience grew quiet. Her voice resounded across the space. Everyone could hear clearly.

"We Noor are merely caretakers of the known Universe; not meant to rule it, but to guide it. The Almighty should be your ultimate authority. As servant of such a One, and with that in mind, I speak to the people from Earth, first:

"You have nurtured me through most of my life; I am not inexperienced with your ways. I know human nature, and have given this much thought.

"To quote from your own writings: 'Without love you have nothing! Love is patient, love is kind, and is not jealous...it does not promote itself; does not take into account a wrong suffered... it endures all things; rejoices in truth...Love never fails! Without love you have nothing!'

"Though the peoples of the Forbidden Planet profess to follow these precepts; only a rare few, do."

An awed silence overcame those listening, as they realized, how well, she really did know them. And then, Susa lowered the boom.

"From this moment on, the humans rescued from the Forbidden Planet, will be under the guardianship of the Feline nation...until such time as a suitable overseer of their own kind emerges. At present, none of the former leadership is acceptable. These have too much attitude of entitlement, and privilege, to sufficiently understand the needs of the disadvantaged. The station of Overseer should not be a function by which you gain riches.

"A Feline Overseer has no more than a common warrior or kit, and so it shall be on your new human world..."

Some boos, followed by exclamations of approval came from corners of the listening crowd.

"The Universal Council has decreed; you shall be given a class M planet on which to settle...with stipulations. Your human kind is still primitive, you have too little control over your baser natures, to be trusted among us, without suitable training. All are aware of your uncivilized ways; you are notorious for your lack of morality, dispassionate nature, and greed. There is still much enmity between brother races. You have the potential to become just like the dog creatures who imprisoned you.

"Therefore...you will not be permitted to join in the Federated Alliance; nor will you be given access to Jump services. There will be no interaction with us, and you will be prohibited from developing space travel, until...you have matured to the place where you will not be a danger to other species.

"For the humans who are willing to abide by Universal law, we give you a choice to remain out here, but remember...the punishment for failure to comply with our ways is death; the breaking of law has a cost!"

Everywhere, growls of disbelief, and censure, came from the new human populace, but the Feline Queen ignored them.

"And now, I address the Feline nation itself:

"I have decided to abdicate as Feline leader; like Kei appointed me, I now pass that duty to the pure Feline Dia, of the medical station ship. She is better fit to rule her own kind. I am certain, she will rule well, as she has served as my proxy in my absence, and during my recovery.

"As this will also mean, she takes on the added function of chair to the Universal Council, I step down totally. I stated previously: we Noor are not meant to govern you. We are Healers, and much prefer to operate solely in that area. From this time forward, each species will police itself, with the Universal Council, as before, the final Judicial body.

"We Noor will be available for emergencies, and counsel, as needed, but for now, we head back to our parent planet for respite.

"We bid you a pleasant future..."

Abruptly, all Noor, and those with them, vanished from the platform. Only Dia, and Kimon, were left standing alone in the craft.

Two seconds passed. Then, the Feline guardian warriors, appointed to guard their new Queen, were jumped to Dia's side, as was the new chosen pilot for the controls. While the craft powered up, all pandemonium broke out among the crowd.

A new time had begun; they were on their own!

###

A Guide to knowing the creatures of this tale:

NOOR: a humanoid being with exceptional psychic abilities, the degree varying with each individual. Some also have the capability to separate its mental essence from the physical body.

-In a conjunctive male: the two halves exhibit themselves as two separate physical entities.

example: Liam/Loki

-In an introvert female: the two display as different personalities; only one dominates at a time.

example: Tilk/Susa.

FELINE: man-size intelligent cat beings.

example: Dia, Kimon, Uel

BEAR: a giant bear being-intelligent, protective, used as body guards

ROOT: tree-like beings. Said to have little empathy, a trickster and devious.

example: Theee, More and Zaba

ROOG: large dog-like beings. Not necessarily highly intelligent; very aggressive and predatory.

SLITHER: snake-like creature with chameleon abilities. Also able to remain invisible for long periods of time. Usually a light blue-green, but color darkens when they are about to attack. Only emotions it is capable of are protective instinct and anger-attack. When a Slither emotionally attaches to a being not of their kind, it will protect for life.

example: Oona

BOM: a cross-breed Roog/Feline

LIAM/LOKI: a cross-breed Noor/Feline

Other NOOR/FELINE are: Twila and Jabek; Shiveron and Reon

TUSHA: a HUMAN/NOOR-(tusha is the name for butterfly in the Noor tongue)

Other HUMAN/NOOR: Nyle and Kaudy, Moriah and Iora.

SLITHER/HUMAN: Sith and mate Serene

BEAR/HUMAN: Wadi and mate Rimu

About the Author:

Margaret Afseth, a Canadian novelist, grew up on the prairies. She raised her four children from preschool age to teens on her own. Now, as a widow and grandmother, through the encouragement of her family to follow her dream of writing full time, and publishing her work, she has stepped to the publishing stage in the latter years of her life.

Since her late teens, Margaret was always an avid reader and clandestine writer, but due to discouragement, and the unfortunate hard lesson in which her first novel was destroyed by a misguided counselor, she was too publisher shy to go through the gauntlet of the critics...until, that is, the ease of on line self-publishing became available.

The last novel of the Noor series was written while the author was sight impaired, and recovering from chemo and radiation therapy, due to a cancerous tumor growing behind her eyes. The dedication in this book gives appreciation to her caregivers.

In February 2013 Margaret published her first sci-fi thriller the Aopato Chronicles.

Discover other titles by Margaret Afseth on
Amazon.com

Aopato book 1 (Aopato Chronicles)

Remedy book 2 (Aopato Chronicles)

Turn Back book 3 (Aopato Chronicles)

Hidden From View (a short story)

Gentle Beast-book 1 (Noor Chronicles)

Soul Saver-book 2 (Noor Chronicles)

If you enjoyed this book, here is a sample of the other series.

AOPATO

By

Margaret Afseth

Prologue:

1902 Northern Canada

The settlement consisted of the lumber office, a trading post and the row of connecting log houses everyone called the motel. It was in the cabin, third from the left, that the man and the boy had spent the night.

Inside, the room smelled of alcohol, stale cigarette smoke, dirty socks and urine, which emanated from the chamber pot in the far west corner. Littering a small table, three feet from the dingy bed, were two dirty aluminum plates, two tin cups, one still half full, and pages of newsprint scattered across the top.

It was dim, the window shades drawn.

Sprawled upon the tousled cot was a tall, extremely thin man; his salt and pepper hair matted, his unwashed red chequered shirt ragged, and the coveralls worn. He was shoe less.

In his right hand he held a half empty bottle of cheap whiskey. Near his left hip, a small loaded pistol waited for his courage to be fortified enough that its owner might actually carry out the purpose for which the weapon had been purchased.

The man wondered:

How did I come to this place?

He lifted the bottle to his lips drawing deeply. The amber liquid burned as it travelled down his throat.

First he had killed his favourite son while working in the bush, the tree falling with such finality, ending the child's life before it began. He had felt that last breath leave his slight frame, and as he grieved his loss beside the mounded earth they had come.

The man had seemed just like any other, but it was hard to make out features for the light that shown behind him. In his arms he carried a sleeping boy near the age of Jake's lost son. He offered to give the child to Jake…said that one could take the place of his treasure.

Would Jake take the small one, raise him as his own; keep him safe from something that hunted the child?

Jake had agreed, too numb from his sorrow to think ahead to the consequences such an action would bring.

A night bird called from outside the window. Darkness was closing in.

That child will never replaced my own.

Though he had so resembled his son in face and features, the new one acted strange, different some how, peculiar.

Jake had given the new boy his son's name. *Avery.*

The outside door rattled in the wind.

Is it here? Has it found us at last?

But though he listened hard, only distant sounds of revelry came from outside in the night.

They had travelled together, he and the child, moving from place to place, the man always feeling hunted, though by what he could not tell. They had just kept running.

The bottle found his lips once again, but it did not drown his fear.

I am tired of running; I can do this no longer; I will flee no more. This is over. Finished. Let someone else protect the boy...

He had sent Avery to the store.

"We need supplies," Jake told Avery, handing him money. "Go to the post. Pick up some grub... spend time looking around."

Jake raised the bottle, draining its contents.

The smell of the room was becoming overpowering; added to the usual stench was now the odour of sulphur, rotting flesh; the metallic taste of blood.

The air filled with overwhelming anger, rage; utter viciousness.

It is here! I can feel it!

He could not see anything; never could, only felt the presence of something so evil his heart threatened to stop with the fear.

I will face it this time.

A hollow voice, as though someone breathed through a tube, sounded about him.

Too loud! It was more inside his mind than around him.

"What have you done with him?"

"He's gone," the man answered. "Go find him yourself."

A hard derisive snort, and Jake began to tremble.

"I will kill you first, so you can no longer hide him."

Jake did not care anymore.

Let the creature have its way. I am tired of running; I am ready to die.

Trying to wear him down, drawing out the minutes, the being meant to torture him.

Silence dragged in the room.

Suddenly, without Jake's will or control, his hand released the bottle, and picked up the gun. He raised it to his head, pointed to his temple, pulled back the trigger...and fired.

Simultaneous with the loud report, a blinding flash occurred, flooding the cabin in light. On either side of the room, two small bright star-like orbs appeared in mid air.

Beside the bed, a huge grotesque shape shimmered to visibility, a reptilian creature, reeking of hatred and revenge.

"You will not stop me!" it thundered.

A beam of red light zapped from the reptilian to the star shape on the right, while at the same moment another of blue went from the star at the left to the monster.

The first star object exploded with such force the room went almost dim.

Beside the bed, the ugly being began to melt slowly, as a hot candle melts in extreme heat, turning to dark vapour, then at last fading from sight.

As the outside door began to open, the second star vanished. All went still...and dark.

A slight boy of seven entered, a bag of groceries in his arm.

Avery pondered the darkened room; set his burden in the chair by the door. He made his way to the bedside; fumbled to light the lamp. His hands came away sticky, and wondering why; he turned up the wick.

The scene accosting his senses stunned him. The man upon the bed had only half a face; the pillow beneath him was covered with chunks of brain matter; the faded blue blanket was spattered with bright red blood, as was the yellowing walls. The lamp dripped with dead tissue and gore.

At first he did not comprehend. He raised his hands and pondered them. He looked up, gazing about the room.

It sure stinks in here.

He looked again at the man he knew, sprawled upon the bed. Realization finally hit him; what had just happened in this room; why he had been sent away.

The young boy screamed.

From then on, he entered a world of numbness from which he would never quite recover. As from a distance, his screams continued…on…and on…and on.

Outside alarmed voices called to one another. The door was rammed in hard; it banged against the wall.

Finally, someone was leading him away.

Outside. Fresh air. Someone folded him in comforting arms…

But forever, that memory would visit him in his dreams.

To continue reading please go to Amazon.com to purchase the book.

www.ingramcontent.com/pod-product-compliance
Lightning Source LLC
Chambersburg PA
CBHW021232020726
47498CB00008B/2802